CLOCKS AT CHRISTMAS

and other stories

Bryan Webster

Dedicated to my family, Mary, Mary's family and all the other folk who have made my Christmases times of comfort and joy.

CONTENTS

INTRODUCTION

I love Christmas. Winter would be gie dreich without it.

Over the years I have written a story to mark the season and sent it to a group of friends.

I have now decided to collect them so they may be read at any time. They vary considerably. Some are serious; others, light-hearted.

Almost all are based on real places, people and events. All I have done is to fashion a story from them.

I hope they help you to enjoy Christmas.

Bryan Webster

CLOCKS AT CHRISTMAS

I have two clocks in the front room. They collude. If the mantel clock stops the longcase follows. If they agree to keep going between winds, they do so. But that does not mean they agree on all things. Occasionally I detect a little friction between them. Sometimes one or the other will work on for a little while after the other has gone on strike.

For instance, the mantel clock took to stopping at 12, midday and midnight. This pedantry clearly irritated the longcase clock. It didn't exactly ignore the other but it sulked in its corner for a few hours before joining the protest.

What they were protesting about I do not know but I picked this up just before Christmas last year. See what you make of it.

'Were you thinking of doing anything special for Christmas?' asked Longcase.

'I don't know,' replied Mantel. 'What does he do for Christmas. Does he deck the halls or just sit and sleep?

''Bit of both. He used to do the whole jing-bang: tree, holly, decorations, silly ornaments; hung up his Christmas Cards on the walls here; one string in the corner by the cupboard there, and two over here, one either side of the bookcase.'

'Each!'

'What?'

'It should be each; each side, not either side; it's not a comparative, either-or, it's an alternative: *each* side of the bookcase.'

'Does it matter?'

'It did at Tremlington Hall.'

'Oh, you're bringing that up again. But you know what I meant.'

Mantel kept quiet for a while.

'Anything up beside me - festive garlands, stockings, cotton wool, synthetic snow, candlesticks, that sort of clutter?'

'Not garlands, a bit of holly over the picture there, and candlesticks. He likes his candlesticks.'

'Crystal?'

'No. Used to be brass, but he gave those away. He has a glass pair, with holly and poinsettias painted on them.'

'Glass with painted poinsettias! What? Up here beside me?'

'Used to be. But he threw a lot of stuff out last year after his wife died. She liked Christmas. He didn't have the heart for it.'

'Threw his Christmas stuff out?'

'Well, took them to the Charity shop. There was a suitcase full of them.'

'Tell me the poinsettia candlesticks went with them.'

'Could have been. I can't recall seeing them last year. But you were here last year. Do you not remember?'

'Well, no,' said Mantel dully, and fell silent.

Longcase studied him a moment.

'Of course, sorry, I remember now, you were out of commission. You had had a breakdown.'

'Do you mind? Out of commission! Breakdown! There was no breakdown. I was indisposed. I hadn't been here long. Hadn't got used to the place. No wonder! If you had spent most of your life at Tremlington then found yourself in an end-terrace, you'd be indisposed. He showed no understanding, so what was I to do? Carry on as if nothing had happened?'

'I've been in an end-terrace, this end terrace, for most of my life, and have never felt the need to be indisposed at it.'

'But when you have known splendour, and are then reduced to this....'

'Look, this is a good place, a respectable place - and I've been in better. I didn't start my life here, you know. If you had any sense of quality you would have worked that out. Do you think these common fisherfolk could have afforded my services when I was new? No! I was in the big house. You've seen it. Across the water. Owned by the Nesbitt's, rich men; they could afford a good clock or two.'

'I've heard they made their money smuggling'

'Before my time. And what if they did? How did Lord Tremlington make his pile? Squeezing rents out of the peasants, I should think, or exploiting slaves in Antigua.'

'There was no Lord Tremlington. The family name was Parker-Knowles.'

'I've heard of them. They make armchairs.'

'They do nothing of the sort! That would be well beneath them. They wouldn't touch commercial. They had land, and interests in the city.'

'What about the skip, then? How does that come into it?'

Longcase pronounced this for effect. And what an effect it had.

Mantel shuddered as the sentence hit him and for a moment said nothing. When he replied his voice sounded restrained, not to say, strangled.

'Skip? What skip?'

'I heard you'd been rescued from a skip.'

'Where on earth did you get that from?'

As he said this he attempted a dismissive laugh. It came over as a stifled sob

'Donald, the Clock Doc. When you were under the weather, and under his care. When he first saw you he tutted, and wondered how your bracket got bent. Then he rang the man who sold you to himself - Michael, I think, of Prestigious Clocks, based, if I remember right, on an industrial site in Birmingham. He said that he had not had time to do you up; that you had just been brought in; that you had been found in a skip; that's why himself had got you cheap.'

'Please! Do you not realise how hurtful these allegations are? I am well-bred and not used to this sort of abuse. Have you not read it in my face? I was born to Mappin & Webb, a name perhaps you have not come across, but instantly identified and respected by clock-lovers. What's on your dial: 'J and W Nicholson, Berwick'? Who on earth are they?'

'As it says, clockmakers in Berwick.'

'Not clock MAKERS. They didn't MAKE clocks! They sold them. Put their name on the dial and sold them, that's what Nicholson, or whatever you call them, did. They weren't clock MAKERS.'

'Have it your own way. It's better than being in a skip. And so is this. I've found it a comfortable billet since I was brought here. I was under the weather myself not long before you came. Himself was to blame. Well, partly. I felt off-colour for a couple of weeks, wheezy and a bit stiff in the joints. He applied engine oil. You know the thick sticky stuff. Gummed up the innards, constipation. I soldiered on, but eventually I had to give up. But, credit where it's due, he called in Donald and he put me in dock for a couple of months. Cleaned up all the works, brushed up the bushes, replaced some of the worn-out bits, massaged the old limbs, oiled the joints. After ten weeks I felt as good as new. And himself paid for it all. He could have let me go, but he stood by me, and I'll stand by him.'

'He hasn't done much for me. Just winds me up on a Friday and expects a weeks' work out of me.'

'And he hasn't always had that, has he?'

'What do you mean?'

'Well, I mean this stopping at twelve day and night. Attention seeking, that's all that was.'

'It was not! I wasn't well.'

'You were lucky he didn't give you the heave-ho back into the skip. You mean nothing to him: no history, no connections. I've served the family for, what a hundred and thirteen years, if you count Old Pate.'

'Who on earth was old Pate?'

'Let me see. He was the granny's sister's man. She took him in when her sister died and I came with him. I'm now part of the furniture. No, more than that - part of the establishment. Grandmother's sister's man was a Burgeon. They were big in the town, fish merchants, loaded. It was them that could afford to give me a berth when the big house was broken up. I had to get over that, and you'll have to get over being thrown out of Lord Tremlington's place. It happens to clocks. There's no need to sulk about it.'

. 'There was never a Lord Tremlington, I keep telling you. And I wasn't sulking. It was the heat. It's alright for you over there in the corner, but when that log fire is on, it's, it's, ...'

'Skumfishing', I think, is the word you're looking for.'

'Skumfishing! What on earth does that mean?'

'If I could tell you what it means I wouldn't have to use it. It's what you feel when that fire is belching out heat. It comes from the old reiver practice of smoking the opposition out of their towers. They would pile logs, straw and trees against the wall and then set fire....'

'Alright, save me the lecture. It was too warm. Played havoc with my breathing. I'm sensitive about my breathing.'

'I would have thought Mappin and Webster would have thought about that when they produced you. You're a mantel clock. Mantel Clocks stand on mantel shelves. Mantel shelves are just above fires. Fires get warm.'

'Mappin and Webb, not Webster. Do you know what he did? Do you? I've never been so insulted in my life. He sprayed me with oil.'

'Yes, I saw that. WD40 was what he used. Which is a big improvement on what he used on me.'

'Why didn't he consult the doctor?'

'Couldn't get him. He asked him to take a look at you, but Doc's a busy man. Anyway, it seemed to do the trick. You've never stopped since.'

'Of course, do you think I want dosed with that evil-smelling stuff again. No, no, I'll just have to tick on as best I can.'

He sounded despondent, and I expect the longcase clock, that has seen life in all its ups and downs, felt sorry for him.

'Ay, do that,' he said sympathetically, then added. 'Look, can I say something. It's nice having company. I've stared at that mantelpiece for years and thought it needed something to bring it to life. You've done that. And I must say I like your chime. I've always thought mine was a bit tinny for a tall man, but yours is a fine deep mellow sort of tone.'

'Oh, thank you. Yes, at Tremlington many visitors commented on it. In fact, we once had Prince Edward for the night, and he was particularly complimentary. And then there was Grand Duke....'

Longcase butted in.

'And what about Christmas, then; you're not going to spoil it for him, are you?'

'No,' replied Mantel, 'I have always quite enjoyed Christmas. At Tremlington they made a feature of the clocks at Christmas. And they always had the Messiah. I don't suppose he plays the Messiah, does he?'

'The Messiah! Oh, yes, every Christmas, without fail – and he always tunes into 'Carols from Kings.'

'In which case I'll chime in.'

Then he added, 'But I find it exhausting. I may take a short break afterwards. Would you care to join me?'

'I'll think about it,' said Longcase.

The clocks kept perfect time over Christmas and wore their garlands of ivy without complaint. Their quiet ticking settled a peace on the room and their chimes blessed the whole house with their serenity.

But at midday on the tenth of January the clock on the mantel shelf stopped and I couldn't get it going again. The next morning, I entered a silent room and realised that the longcase clock had also given up. I was about to call the Clock Doc, when I remembered the WD40. I fetched it from the car, but as soon as I entered the room, my ears picked up the sound of ticking. Both clocks had started up again. And have gone on faultlessly ever since.

Christmas 2016

CHRISTMAS ALONE

Now that his two sisters had fallen out, Raymond could see his way to a happy Christmas. He'd be able to spend it on his own; something he had longed for since his wife left him eleven years ago. Or, if he were honest, what he had longed for long before that.

Nowadays, he could not think of any good reason why he had married Morven. They were never engaged, nor could he remember proposing to her. She had been part of the same crowd that used to hang around together in Shipcote, a suburb of Gateshead on Tyneside. The other youths and lasses seemed to pair off, until only he and Morven were left, so they got into bed together and, after a few years, married.

If you asked him now whether he ever liked Morven, he would tell you that he must have done - well enough to marry her, anyway, but he can't remember ever having done so. He is certain, however, that she didn't like him. He didn't particularly like himself; on that subject he has no fixed opinion.

Perhaps that is not surprising. Would you not agree that the opinion slapped on us at school sticks on us for the rest of our lives? I know that, in my school report, the headmaster, Horatio B. Bates of blessed memory, scribbled at the foot of a page of poor results: *'he is inclined to avoid anything that requires much effort'*. It's a fair description, I would say.

But not one that applied to Raymond. He stuck in at everything that was placed in front of him – so long it was in a book and he had ruled paper to write on. Effort made up most of his store of ability and his exam results always hovered around six-and-a-half and seven - except in arithmetic where he occasionally recorded an eight.

His abilities determined his future career or, perhaps, we should call it, series of jobs. Leaving school, the Labour Exchange pointed him in the direction of clerical work and he tracked his way in that trade through a number of shops, factories and offices most of which you will no longer find listed in any business directory. However, for the last twenty-five years of his working life, he took the bus across the Tyne to report each day to Lowrie and Lowther, Chartered Accountants, in The Chare, Newcastle.

His home, however, no longer lay in the bustling streets of Gateshead. Now he lived in row of quiet farm cottages not far from Lowick in the north of Northumberland. It was Morven's idea to move there seeing that they were approaching retirement. For a few years he drove their clapped-out car to Berwick from whence he took the train to Newcastle. Then, one day, he came back to the family home, to find it empty. Well, not completely empty; she had left a table, one dining chair, one armchair and the single bed in which he had slept since she objected to his snoring. At the time of his banishment, she said that she had come to the country for a quiet life but how could she enjoy it when, every night, she had to sleep in the same room as an intermittent chain saw. Strictly speaking we should not be calling it a family home for they had no children, but 'connubial nest' doesn't quite answer the need for an accurate description.

As we said earlier, that disruption now lay twelve years in the past. Raymond had retired from the accountants with a Moorcroft Vase, small pension and a speech from old Mr Lowther commending him for his reliability and painstaking meticulousness. He lived modestly in the old farm cottage. He had acquired a cat called Ollie and found in it most of the company he desired. On Wednesday evenings, he walked a mile and a half into the village to take part in the weekly pub quiz at The Leg of Mutton; on Saturdays, he took the bus to Berwick to do his shopping, and on Sunday, Mrs Allen, the farmer's wife, picked him up and drove him to Lowick Parish Church to attend Divine Worship.

What he enjoyed most about Christmas; well, his present experience of Christmas, lay largely in his tabulation of Christmas cards. For the past twelve years, having for that period full control over their receipt and despatch, he had recorded meticulously to whom he sent cards and from whom he received them. Not only that; he noted the subject depicted on each card and cross-referenced them.

If you show sufficient interest, he will tell you that the incidence of nativity scenes has decreased at the same rate as robins have increased, more or less. Which trend he puts down to the materialisation of Christmas. Being a touch old-fashioned and a regular churchgoer, in his own purchases, year on year, he seeks to shift the emphasis back to religious themes. But what is one man against attuned and avaricious card manufacturers?

However interesting this may be, it is not the point of our story, so with apologies, I will leave it and return to his anticipation of a comfortable Christmas with only the cat for company.

Why his sisters had fallen out he did not know and had no interest in finding out. He liked them both. He didn't care for their husbands, and suspected that, in their respective spouses, lay the root of his sisters' disagreement. Harold, Gladys' man, was a braggart. In Prestige Boilers and Heat Engineering, he had risen to become Area Manager (North-East) and had abandoned the terraces of Deckham for the treelined avenues of Low Fell. He thus regarded his own trajectory in life as successful. This led him to despise anyone who had settled for working class contentment, such as Grace's other half, Maurice. He had spent, and still spent, his days delivering miscellaneous packages for miscellaneous firms in a white van.

Whenever the two men met for any length of time, Maurice would vow never to sit in the same room as Harold again, and Harold would tell Gladys that if he were Grace, he would give Maurice the elbow. You can understand that this did not make for happy family get-togethers.

The feast rotated round the three homes: Gladys laid it on it one year, Grace the next, then Raymond. This Christmas was to have been his turn. The sisters, accompanied by their husbands, would have driven from Tyneside in order to sit round a festive board that they had largely brought with them, the two women having correctly assumed that Raymond, left to himself, would not be capable of putting on the table a meal that matched the occasion.

Whether in this lay the cause of the fall-out, Raymond could not be sure, but at the last Christmas lunch in his house, he thought he had heard a rather tight discussion between Gladys and Grace about whether his contribution met the full expense of the dinner. He had raised the matter with them, but they had both assured him that they were quite happy with what he paid. At the time he was reassured but when they called off this year he suspected that the grumble had been not so much about what he chipped in but about how it had been divvied up between them.

Whatever had caused the rift, this year's get together had been cancelled by mutual consent of his sisters. They would not be coming for lunch on Christmas Day.

Of course, Raymond had expressed regret when Gladys told him but, in good heart, set about preparing a feast to his own recipe. In the morning he would attend the ten-thirty service at the church with Mrs Allan, in the afternoon he would go for a long walk in the brisk winter air and in the evening he would first of all put the finishing touches to his Christmas Card statistics then break out a bottle of ginger wine, heat a mince pie, put on 'It's a Wonderful Life', and fall asleep watching it. And lunch? Mrs Allen had invited him to the farm, but he would provide for himself. This scratched another itch. His sisters always brought what suited them and he paid for it; he didn't get to choose. Well, this year he would eat what he liked, and he had seen something he fancied in Marks and Spencer: a frozen Traditional Christmas Dinner: Turkey, stuffing, baked potatoes and all the trimmings; with Christmas Pud and white sauce to follow. On Christmas Eve, as he settled in his chair before his log fire, he looked forward to the great day with a sense of warm anticipation.

The Vicar spoiled it. That's trouble with these young radicals. Instead of the old story properly cast and furnished with manger, star, a cluster of shepherds, three wise men and the cattle lowing, he majored on peace on earth, or rather the lack of it, due to 'our own selfish attitudes'. Like wanting to spend Christmas on our own!

The vicar did not actually use this last sentence but Raymond heard it in his heart and it made him feel guilty – and mean. He went back home and attempted to resurrect his enthusiasm for a solitary celebration. But it would not return and, the more he tried, the more he learned that what had enticed him was the *prospect* of such a day. Now that it had arrived, he understood perfectly that the *reality* would not measure up to the vision. He found himself in uncharted territory; he had not enjoyed or, as it now weighed on his mind, 'endured' a Christmas on his own before. He looked at the clock; the day was not yet half over. The sun shone, the air crisp. Perhaps a walk would restore his spirits.

Three miles he walked, along quiet roads, beside resting fields and sleeping woods. With every step he encouraged his appetite to look forward to his M & S Traditional Christmas Dinner. But the glory had departed. Was the sun sinking so early? As he neared his cottage, he no longer relished his lonely meal.

When he turned the corner of the row, however, he spotted a car drawn up outside his home; a car he recognised. It can't be them, can it?

'We couldn't go without seeing you on Christmas Day,' explained Gladys. 'So, we left Maurice to make the dinner and we came here for lunch. On the way we sorted out things between us. Grace glanced at her sister, smiled and added,

'We've brought three packets of Marks and Spencer's Traditional Christmas Dinner. We can heat them up in the microwave. It's not much but…'

Raymond interrupted her.

'That'll be very nice,' he said.

Christmas 2020

IT COULD HAVE BEEN THE WIND

This one is prompted by the old twelfth century church at Ancroft, not far from Berwick-on-Tweed. I am easily persuaded that there is something magical at work at Christmas.

Of course, it could have been the wind. The vicar told the bishop it was defiance, but it could have been the wind.

There was a wind that night. Mrs Nelson said as much when she told me the story many years ago. But she didn't believe it was the wind. Indeed, she partly agreed with the vicar. It was defiance, she said, but not by us; we didn't touch the bell.

It was a cold night, she reported, as expected on the 24th of December; Christmas come in the cold dark dying of the year. It came every year like that to the village of Barton; not really a village, a bleak huddle of houses straggling round the junction where the old drove road from Thornton met the main road from Langlee to Gainslaw. The road bent sharply as it came through the village, slicing the business end of the village from its ancient religious roots.

The business end! No longer! All business gone, leaving only an empty street and dilapidated buildings: the forlorn village hall, the converted school (now an unsatisfactory house; 'For Sale' for two and half years), the corrugated garage (a rusting hulk fronted by two gaunt pumps), the old Mains farm (house long gone; sheds only - used for bale storage and wintering cattle); a severe terrace of empty labourers' houses (alive only when housing the homeless, courtesy of an accommodating estate or intervening social worker); the old Post Office (the shop closed, the counter gone; now a house only, the home of Mrs Nelson, ex-postmistress, purveyor of local stories, she who told me about the bell).

But the ancient church still stood, and, in spite of the vicar, held to its old occupation. The vicar saw no need for services at Barton; the Mock-Gothic parish church at Gainslaw only five miles away could easily accommodate the remnant who insisted on worshipping at Barton.

Set back into the angle of the main road, the church squatted amongst the yew trees and gravestones that populated the churchyard. A sign on the main road directed visitors to it: *"Ch: 12ᵗʰ c."* If any wanted to visit the church (and not many did) a short lane flanked by a high stone wall brought them to the gate of the church. Over the wall lay the old rectory, and we need to notice it for it plays a bit-part in Mrs Nelson's story.

It no longer housed a rector, or priest, or any other ecclesiastic, but a property developer from Newcastle when he was there, which was not often. He came with a house party two or three times a year, and always at Christmas to play the Squire at Home. He had insisted early in his tenure that the bell be silenced. He had a point - the bell rang too loud for the size of the church, or the village for that matter, and it lay next to his house. To claim, as he did, that the bell shook the foundations may be an exaggeration, but, certainly, it rattled the Meissen in his china cabinet.

The silencing of the bell suited the vicar. In addition to his aversion for his Barton flock, he did not like the bell and, truth to tell, it was easy to dislike. As well as being loud it sounded flat; it clanged rather than rang and had no indemnifying antiquity. Canon Potts, an eccentric predecessor had had it installed in 1862 in the expectation that the entire parish would hear it, and the parish lay wide and scattered. Certainly, the people at Thornton, three miles away, claimed they could make it out when the wind blew from the East. That it shook the Rectory had not bothered Canon Potts. He lived in The Rectory and owned the bell.

At the time of Mrs Nelson's story, the parish, for ten years, had been linked with Gainslaw from whence the vicar sallied forth each Sunday to conduct matins. He found it disheartening. Any slight spiritual uplift he had gained from worshipping in goodly company in centrally heated Gainslaw Gothic quickly dissipated in the cool sweet smell of dry rot at Barton.

There he looked out on five people. Mr & Mrs Nesbitt, a retired farmer and his wife, kept faith with their forebears whose memorials tableted the walls. Mrs Ancroft, a gracious old lady, made her way from the retirement bungalow she had shared with her husband. He now lay in the churchyard and therefore, it could be said, continued to attend the means of grace; certainly, it gave Mrs Ancroft a little comfort to think so. Jimmy Deans also attended; a simple man, useful to farmers in the days when fieldwork had to be done by man's hand; redundant for many years, his work usurped by machines he could not master. He loved his church for there he had learnt that he was a prince of the Kingdom of Heaven. He used to ring the bell but now contented himself with tidying the churchyard and taking up the collection.

Mrs Nelson completed the little flock. She organised what needed organising, coaxed a tune out of the wheezy organ, and tenaciously resisted any attempt of the vicar, bishop or dry rot to close the church.

Christmas! Time for greenery, jollity, piety, singing and bells! But no bell at Barton, not even to welcome in Christmas Day. The vicar, aware of the tenacity of Mrs Nelson and the perversity of his flock, each Sunday in Advent expounded on the environmental significance of silence from the bell.

Indeed, if he could have prevented it, there would be no Watchnight Service on Christmas Eve. He could see no need of it; the whole congregation could comfortably fit into one pew at Gainslaw Gothic to take part in the Municipal Midnight Mass there. (Generous man that he is, he even offered to lay on transport). But no, they wanted their own service; the argument, as submitted by Mrs Nelson, being that some stranger, seeking solace, might turn up only to find the church cold, dark and locked against them. They would therefore conduct the service themselves: Mr Nesbitt leading, Mrs Nelson playing and the others doing their best with lessons layered with carols.

The church would be decorated of course - with holly, yew and ivy, a candle here and there, and, on the font, a flower arrangement in red, white and gold; another would give welcome in the porch. But there would be no bell, no bell to announce to the far-flung parish that the Light of the World had come again in the cold darkness of midwinter.

There were strangers in the village, strangers from a far country: East European, anonymous, man, woman and infant child, living in the austere terrace. He laboured in the vegetable processing plant at Thornton; there to provide a better living for his family than he could earn in the old country. His wife had seen and half-understood the notice of the Watchnight Service that Mrs Nelson had pinned in the glass-fronted notice board that shivered in the wind outside the old village hall. It brought to her mind the quiet joy of Christmases past among folk she knew.

That Christmas Eve at half-past eleven, Mrs Nelson told me, it was biting cold, with flecks of snow in a rising East wind. Mr Nesbitt stood in the mouth of the chancel, two stairs up from the congregation that sprinkled the church. The Squire host and his guests from the old rectory also attended, taking in the service as part of their Country Christmas Experience; eight of them, bright, lively, inattentive, sitting wrapped up at the front of the nave, on the pulpit side.

Mr Nesbitt, at the lectern takes out his pocket watch, looks at it, replaces it, clears his throat and begins:

> *The people that walked in darkness have seen a great light*
> *They that dwell in the land of the shadow of death*
> *Upon them hath the light shined*

The service proceeds, a sandwich of lessons and carols, until, before the last hymn, a suitable, seasonal, short poem from Mr Nesbitt:

> *Christmas Eve and twelve of the clock.*
> *'They'll be all on their knees,'*
> *Said an elder as we sat in a flock*

Round the embers in hearthside ease."

"But we got through it too fast", reported Mrs Nelson. "It was six minutes yet to midnight. Poor Mr Nesbitt looked over to me. I motioned to him to stand still and wait for twelve o'clock. Only then could we sing *'O Come all Ye'*, including the last verse".

"You cannot sing that," explained Mrs Nelson, "except on Christmas Day."

Mr Nesbitt hovered like an uncertain angel, watch in hand, waiting for midnight. In the old days, before the bell was silenced, there would have been no need for the watch; Jimmy Deans kept the time. He clanged out the hour when it arrived. Then they could sing the hymn.

The church fell silent, Mrs Nelson recounted. She heard the wind scuttling around the roof and bustling at the windows. Each one in their pew sat quietly, even the house party. Three long minutes ticked by; longer for Mr Nesbitt than anyone else.

Then, said Mrs Nelson, the church door rattled and everyone jumped in their seats. Slowly the door creaked open and a young man and woman entered, the woman carrying her baby. Mrs Nelson recognised them as the potato packer and his wife from the terrace and left her stool to scuttle down the aisle to usher them to a pew at the front of the church.

But before the woman would sit down she stopped, and cradling her child, faced the altar and dropped her knee in genuflection. Then, then, as the people watched and listened, to the astonishment of them all: Mrs Nelson, Mr Nesbitt and his wife, Mrs Ancroft the widow, Jimmy the labourer, the Squire and all his guests, each in their own pew standing stock still, listening and staring, the bell tolled, filling the church to every corner with a loud, flat, consoling clang. Mr Nesbitt looked at his watch. Midnight! Christmas Day!

"Yea, Lord we greet thee, born this happy morning'

By the end of the hymn the bell had ceased. When, at the end of the service, Mrs Nelson unlocked the door to the bell-tower and led the curious congregation into it they found the bell rope swinging, but no one there.

Of course, it could have been the wind.

Christmas 2009

TWELVE DAYS OF CHRISTMAS

I wrote this story after I heard of a local young mother who, faced with the same decision as the woman in the story, made the same choice.

'So, he's not going tae dae it?' said Jimmie the beadle to the Session Clerk.

'Didn't even let me get started,' replied Mrs Henderson.

'Did ye explain the circumstances? It would mean a lot to the lassie – and her man'.

'No, as I've said, wouldn't let me get started. Cut me off as soon as I mentioned christening. 'No,' he said, 'You should know by now that I don't baptise children of those who don't come to church."

'He wouldn't have said that twenty years ago,' mumbled Jimmy, mostly to himself.

''What was that?' asked Mrs Henderson.

'Oh, nothing,' said Jimmie and switched the subject to the advent candle holder in his hand.

'This year he wants them to reflect the migrant crisis.'

'That was last year, wasn't it?' said the Session Clerk.

'No,' mumbled Jimmie, 'last year it was the pandemic, with special emphasis on those who have no access to medical care and adequate health facilities.'

As he pronounced the sentence in best Edinburgh English, Mrs Henderson smiled, recognising the sort of cluttered sentence much used by the Rev Dr Eric Cathcart, their minister.

Twenty-five years ago, Dr Cathcart (and he preferred to addressed that way) had arrived as parish minister in Lumsdaine ablaze with evangelical fervour. Replete with divinity degree and doctorate, articulate, resourceful and intelligent, young and vigorous, nothing, he felt, stood in the way of establishing a thriving church of dedicated believers. It had not turned out that way.

Now, as Jimmie recognised, the fire had gone out. Not that Dr Cathcart would admit to it. As far as he believed, he still burned with the vision of a world made new. But the fire that consumed him was more of the gas stove and electric fire; modern, mature, manageable, he would call it. He had given up trying to convert individuals and now channelled his energies into saving the world through projects. It is, after all, much more appealing to persuade colleagues at meetings in 121 George Street of the need to support a food distribution centre in The Gambia, than it is to visit Mrs George in her dingy flat in Frobisher Street and hear again how her man cheated on her and left her penniless.

Here I must plead with you not to be too hard on the man. He had put his best into creating a little Kingdom of God in Lumsdaine, but people had not responded. They had given him attention, respect, support, a regular income and comfortable manse in which to bring up his family. But not what he wanted.

Ask him now what that is and he cannot rightly put a name to it. Back then, when he was thirty, he knew. It was full commitment to Christ; a burning enthusiasm to win people to the Christian Faith. But not many had bought it, and his enthusiasm and energy had dwindled as the years passed.

At first, he would do anything for anyone. (Ask the same Mrs George who drove her a hundred and fifty miles to see her dying mother.) He conducted funerals for sinners and saints alike and baptised any child of any mother that asked him. All this he did to impress the folk of Lumsdaine that 'the town is my parish'; 'I minister to all, not just to churchgoers.'

I am pretty sure that he was taught such noble principles at Trinity College but we must remember that none of his parishioners have had the same benefit. Very soon he found that they took a much less exalted view of the duties of their minister. He featured on their shopping list not as someone who could lead them to a fuller, richer, more committed religious life, but as one who could help them when they couldn't help themselves: with a reference for their school leaver, filling in Social Security forms, and, of course, weddings, funerals and christenings.

Within ten years such utilitarianism sickened him, within fifteen, he had pulled down the shutters. He no longer sought out those in need, He would do what he could to help, if asked, but he announced that he would no longer be available on Saturdays and Mondays. He continued to conduct funerals, and would marry couples if they confessed to being Christians and undertook a short preparation course. But christenings? Only for the children of church members. For, as he would explain to anyone brave enough to ask him, christening, (or as it should be described Infant Baptism) is not about sticking a name on a child and a party, but a ceremony welcoming them into the fellowship of believers – of *believers*.

You will readily understand, that Dr Cathcart approached the Season of Goodwill with barely contained disgust. 'A tinsel show' he called it. 'Robbed of substance and significance by frivolity and sentimentality.'

Such a sentiment made life difficult for Jimmie the Beadle. He found himself caught between the congregation's desire for more display and the minister's abhorrence of it. This year, in particular, he had dreaded asking Dr Cathcart if 'it would be alright' to put the inflatable nativity scene outside the church for the Sundays in Advent.

It was a rumbustious affair: three tubular wise men replete with crowns, rich robes and turbans stood alongside a couple of plump shepherds, one holding a smiling lamb, all surrounding a stable housing a chuffed-looking Joseph, his chubby arm round the shoulders of a serene Mary clutching a swaddled baby. Above them all a bulbous yellow star swung back and forward in the wind. Its glorious absurdity induced everyone passing it to smile. The display irritated Dr Cathcart almost beyond endurance, yet, as Jimmie will tell you, but, is afraid to tell the minister, a nativity tableau was his idea in the first place.

Dr Cathcart had, once more, through gritted teeth, agreed to the humiliation. But enough was enough, he would not countenance this silly request to inveigle him into the charade by christening a baby on Christmas Eve.

We must not, however, believe that such shrivelling of his faith had gone unnoticed by Eric, for behind the title and sophistication there is a man. At first, his rationalisations satisfied his conscience. His reason for denying 'opportunist christenings' he found particularly satisfying. Surely he was justified in denying the right of entry into the church to those who had no intention of joining it. However, as the spontaneous care of his early shepherding gave way to studied bureaucracy, he found that the walls he had built to hem in his flock, also fenced him from his God. His faith had turned cold; and he knew it. He had become an unhappy man.

What part Jimmie played in Dr Cathcart's disquiet, we may not know fully, but certainly, Jimmy's unquestioning goodness repeatedly challenged the minister's scepticism about his parishioners.

'We're all miserable sinners,' he'd say, when the minister complained of some fresh deceit. 'But our God remembers that we are dust.'

What did that mean? Mere sentiment! Yet . . ..

Jimmie had almost finished the Advent Ring when the minister came into the Session Room to inspect it.

'D'ye want words on it this year,' he said. 'Jessie said she'd embroider something if you wanted it.'

'Yes, thank you – and thank her. Could it be 'A Chance for Life'

'A chance for life,' repeated Jimmie and, taking out a ball point pen, made to scribble the words into the small notebook he pulled from his shirt pocket.

The minister watched his beadle expecting Jimmie to ask what the slogan meant. Jimmie finished his writing and put away his book.

'It's about migrants,' explained the minister realising that Jimmie wasn't going to ask.

'Is it?' he replied. 'And how is that?'

The minister warmed to the exposition of a loftier Christmas than that bobbing around in the wind outside.

'I read that a small boat was found off Brighton packed with migrants from Sub-Sahara Africa. One woman was clutching a child of no more than a few months. Yet the authorities were planning to turn them away, until the agency intervened. The woman said she wanted to give her child 'a chance for life'. They must be welcomed, d'ye not think; isn't that the spirit of Christmas?'

Jimmie stared at the minister with an intensity Dr Cathcart had not seen before. For a moment he said nothing then, then spat out,

'It is. Like the lassie's bairn ye willna christen.'

The minister snorted, 'Jimmie, I think I've made it clear. .. '

He got no further. Jimmie cut in.

'Ye're a hard man, Eric, she's giving her bairn a chance at life. And you'll no sprinkle a puckle water on him and gie him a name.'

This was new. It had been years since Jimmie called him by his name. And what was this about a chance at life?

'You'd better explain, Jimmy', he said brusquely.

Jimmy did explain. Virginia, the mother, had long longed for a child, and, at last, had been told that she was expecting a boy. However, as the weeks advanced, the gynaecologist detected a heart defect in the child. Twenty weeks in, he came to the conclusion that the child had a defective heart. Hopefully once the baby was born they could fix it. Then two weeks later he confirmed that part of the child's heart was missing and could not be repaired. At the moment, the child was drawing on the mother's heart. When born he would no longer be able to do that. The gynaecologist advised abortion.

Virginia and her partner thought about it for one night only, then asked the gynaecologist if the bairn would live at all once he was born.

'Yes,' he said, 'about twelve days.'

'Then we will give him a chance at life,' she said.

As Jimmie unfolded the tale, Eric Cathcart's heart broke then warmed.

On Christmas Sunday, the bairn, dressed in his own new baby clothes, was handed, by his father, to Dr Cathcart to be christened.

'Name this child,' he asked Virginia.

'Christmas,' she said.

Note: *The real baby lived and was loved for a few short weeks, then died. Two years later, his mother gave birth to fine, healthy baby boy, who is prospering.*

Christmas 2021

OUR FIRST CHRISTMAS

I wrote this piece in 2015. In that year, in the summer, I had lost Mary, my wife and companion in life.

I remember our first Christmas.

We had married in the August and I had taken up my new charge a fortnight later - in Darlington, a town centre church, a big change from the little Bethel at Hecklescar, a fishing village in the Scottish Borders where I had ventured into the ministry.

There my wife Mary had been born and brought up. A bigger change for her, leaving behind her home, her family, her job, her friends to hazard a life with a tearaway minister anxious to change the world.

The manse was a big brick house just inside the better bit of town, A big brick house with high, draughty rooms, poky living room and cold kitchen. But the lounge was impressive - like something out of a Dickens' hostelry. The room ran the width of the house, from front to back with small paned windows at each end to give it the feel of an old coaching inn. And the fire! It was set into what can only be called an ingle neuk, but it was no nook: it took up at least two-thirds of the wall it inhabited. The fireplace itself was fussily Victorian, overlooking a tiled apron and in turn overlooked by a noble mantelshelf, a mantelshelf crying out for garlands, cards and candlesticks with all of which it was now furnished. A room built for Christmas and we would spend our first Christmas in it.

Not that we'd be on our own. Although this was our first Christmas in our first home Mary had insisted that my mother should join us. A widow of ten years she lived alone but would not be alone at Christmas. Mary, although separated from her own family for the first time, would not tolerate any other arrangement than that we should have my mother with us at Christmas.

My mother then was sixty-five and seemed to me an elderly woman, although a lively one. Now from a vantage point well beyond that milestone, it does not seem to me so very far along the road.

On Christmas Eve we attended the midnight service, where I had tried once again to capture the wonder and mystery of Christmas, and had once again failed. Nevertheless,. the folk streaming out of the church generously wished their new minister, his wife and his mother a happy Christmas, and we all stepped out into a cold, dark, dull night, eager for home and our own firesides.

While Mary retreated to the kitchen to heat up ginger wine and cut the Christmas cake, I stoked up the fire and settled my mother into a fireside chair. Waiting for Mary, I went to the window to look out on the bleak night, to take comfort perhaps, that we were not out there but snug by our own bright hearth..

But when I looked out I saw immediately that it was snowing. Flakes swirled in the streetlights, scurried around the dimly-lit garden and fluttered against the window as if trying to get in out of the cold. I called my mother over and just then Mary stepped through the door carrying the tray with three glasses and three plates of cake. Just outside the window there grew a cotoneaster that, had I been a better gardener, should have been cut back. Now its bright red berries on spindly stalks, iced with snow, chattered and jiggled at the window, a living Christmas card. The snow, the wine, the cake, the fire in the hearth, the dancing bright berries, all combined into a symphony of delight. Mary put down the tray and the three of us, children again, gazed and caught in our very hearts the truth of Christmas as only children know it.

Sitting at home fifty-one years later I still enjoy the thrill of that first Christmas although tears are in my eyes. My mother has been dead these twenty years and more. My wife, my beloved Mary, my companion in life, died in June this year, six long months ago.

But as I sit by the fire I recall that first Christmas. And the remembrance of it warms me more than a little.

24 December 2015

CHRISTMAS FOR A MAN WHO SELLS MATTRESSES.

There's not much in Christmas for a man that sells mattresses. Not even for a one called Joseph.

There again, no one calls me Joseph, not even the wife. She calls me Bud. Bud was the name of the boyfriend she had before she met me and couldn't get out of the way calling me Bud, so after a while I just accepted it. When we married, at the ceremony, when the vicar asked her if she'd have Joseph as her lawful married husband, she asked him to repeat it, then realised he meant me. We have a laugh about it now.

We've been together thirty-seven years and she still calls me Bud. Which is confusing because son Bud is Bud as well. He gets young Bud, though he's not young, not now; he's thirty-five. He's not in mattresses, even though I offered to bring him into the firm. He joined the Air Force and is a Flight Lieutenant. He's the oldest. Then there's Samantha, she's thirty-three, married to a Blackett's manager in Shropshire, so we don't see much of her and her bairns, except at holidays in the summer. Then Buddleia came along as a shock when the missus was forty-two. I didn't want to call her Buddleia; I said it made her sound like a plant. But the wife said she wanted to call her Buddleia; after me, she said. I suggested Josephine, but the wife wanted Buddleia so that's what she is. Mind you, nobody calls her Buddleia; she gets Leia. She helps me in the shop. The wife used to help me, but gave it up when Leia showed an interest.

She's coming on well, is Leia, and is already au fait with mattresses. She can recognise a mattress now just by poking it or sitting on it. We play a little game when we're quiet (which is most of the time). I cover up the labels, then ask her to identify the make and model.

'That's a Silentnight Gellex Select,' she'll say, 'and this is a Myers Morpheus Memory.' She's seldom wrong, but I stymied her the other day with an old Sealy Pocket Sprung. To be fair, it wasn't one of ours so she couldn't recognise it. I'd taken it in in part-exchange.

I sometimes take old mattresses in part exchange just to lubricate the sale. Not that I do anything with them. You can't sell them on. I mean, you wouldn't buy a second-hand mattress, would you? You don't know who's been on them, or what has been, (let us say) deposited, on them. So, I dispose of them environmentally and give the customer a discount; the discount I would have given them anyway, without the trade-in. But they are not to know that – and it gets the mattress out of their way. We don't want them dumped in a layby; bad for the trade that; bad image. Last year I saw a Sealy King Size Firm Sprung dumped in amongst trees up the road. One of the best, the Sealy King Size; expensive too.

Mind you, I would say Leia's expertise lies more along the lines of pillows and cushions. A few months back she sold two memory foam pillows to a man that hadn't had a decent night's sleep for two years, since he cricked his neck. He came back with his wife to thank Leia. It was like a miracle, he said; he was sleeping the whole night through and could still turn his head in the morning. His wife thanked Leia too, saying he was much easier to live with now. He'd become very irritable when he couldn't sleep.

That's what people forget. The world would be a much better place if everyone got a good night's sleep. I've read a few life stories of famous people. It's amazing how many of the evil ones were poor sleepers. Did you know Hitler hardly slept a wink at night – nor Stalin? Margaret Thatcher could do with only three hours, but would you class her as evil? I suppose it depends on your politics. Michael Foot was bad too. Used to sleep on the floor sometimes.

I was explaining this to the vicar at church last week, pointing out that maybe if Herod had had an interior sprung mattress, he wouldn't have been so hard on the children. The vicar smirked and I think he might have been laughing at me under his breath.

That's typical. People think mattresses are funny – or sleazy. They snigger when you say what you do. Yet mattresses are interesting. Did you know that they have found a mattress that is over 70,000 years old? Just a collection of leaves in a little bed, but it shows that down the ages people have welcomed a good night's sleep. Then came straw and feathers; goose feathers were particularly popular. Then, of course, great strides were made when they started making them with springs; interior sprung mattresses. They were the high technology of their day, and they've been refined ever since. Now, of course, you can have memory foam. SlumberWell are working on one that monitors your sleep patterns and remembers what configuration gives you the deepest sleep.

I told the woman that runs U3A that I could give a talk on 'A Good Night's Sleep through the Ages'. I thought that title would grab the attention, but she didn't take it up. Yet I see on the syllabus she has a woman down to talk on 'Cakes, Then and Now'. Now I would have thought that while cakes are interesting, mattresses are essential.

SlumberWell's latest is the YouMatt. When I'm selling one of those, I always get the other half to lie on the bed as well as the client, because it's no use him being comfortable if she isn't, or him - if it's a she - or whoever – the other half; you can never tell nowadays. It's important that they're comfortable as well; otherwise, resentment might creep in.

But nobody wants to buy a mattress at Christmas. We find March and September are the best months. But not December. Then, of course, there's the expense; all the spare money goes on Christmas shopping and there's none left for essentials like mattresses. Though I remember a few years ago a woman coming in on Christmas Eve to buy a new mattress for the 'auld bugger', who turned out to be her father. He'd been over-indulging and had come in feeling cold, so, to warm the bed up, he'd put the electric fire upside down under the blankets. When he came to get in the bed, the fire had burned its way through the mattress to the bed springs. So, she was after a new mattress urgently – as she would. She bought a SilentNight Comfort Plus with 25% off.

The reason I'm telling you all this at Christmas time, is that I suggested to the vicar that I make up a little mattress for the crib at Christmas - for the one he puts outside the church. But he didn't take me on - even when I said I would dispense with the discreet advert I had in mind. It had to be straw, he said he thought, to be genuine. I asked him if he would like to sleep on smelly straw, but he didn't reply. He just said, like he always says, 'Leave it with me and I'll get back to you.' But he never does. It just fades away. The crib went outside without him coming back to me. He'd left it to the last minute and couldn't find any straw, so the doll, er, the Christ Child, was laid on a lump of old woolly blanket. How genuine is that?

So, you can see that there's not much in Christmas for a man that sells mattresses. But that doesn't mean we won't enjoy it. Leia baked some mince pies and we offered any customers that came in a drink of ginger wine and a mince pie. But there weren't many takers, just a woman wanting a pillow to give the dog for its Christmas. So, we ate the mince pies ourselves and closed early.

Anyway, have a Merry Christmas. Sleep Easy. Sleep Well.

December 2018

CHRISTMAS AT BIRSETT (EXTRACT FROM 'ON SUCH A TIDE')

The Birsett of the title is Burnmouth, the first village on the A1 after it crosses the Border. I used it as the location of my first novel, 'On Such a Tide'.

My wife, Mary, was the teacher at the school there and helped to lay on the play performed by the children at Christmas. When we returned to Eyemouth years later we were delighted to find that the tradition had been maintained and expanded. The evening, very much as described in this extract, encapsulates all that a Christmas celebration should be. Unfortunately, the local authority got their way and the school is now closed.

C hristmas, like a bonfire on a dark night, threw forward its light and warmth onto the winter village. It touched the council houses first. A Christmas tree appeared in the window of no. 10 Upper Birsett, then lights in the upstairs window of 15, then the bare rowan at 21 sprouted glowing red fruit. Like a gathering frost the light spread sparkling through whole village: more trees in more windows; in others, light arches with mechanical flickering candlelight; frantic flashing trees appeared outside front doors and, tied to the knockers, wreaths of holly, fir, and synthetic fibre with plastic cones and artificial fruit. Windows normally blind with lined curtains were left open to welcome nosy neighbours and passing strangers to cosy firesides and decorated rooms.

The Great Spirit of the season leaked along the Hecklescar road to the bungalows and villas and at Dam Brezi transformed a spindly hedge into a reindeer with a red nose. Down the brae it ran (the Spirit, not the reindeer), past Mr Scott's, Coastguard's Row and the kirk to cottages by the harbour, then along the road at the foot of the cliff; touching each house, stopping only when it had blessed them all. Number One Partan Row received it last and placed in the window a silver tree bearing golden fruit and, on the front patio, for Ben's sake, an eight-foot tree flashed bright defiance to a sullen winter's sea.

Up the brae, Dot and Spot icicled the eaves of the village hall with light and Melinda the artist decked three of the six lampposts with five-foot hangings of the Kings, the Shepherds and the Holy Family in gold, red and flaming orange. At the school, snowmen, robins and Christmas trees of all shapes and sizes cluttered windows peppered with cotton wool snow. At Birsett Inn, a board outside proclaimed:

'Festive Lunches: Smoked Salmon; Turkey and all the Trimmings; Christmas Pudding/Sherry trifle; Mince Pies: £8.95; Coffee & mints: £1.50; Free Bottle of Wine with every Meal for 4.'

And the new owners hung an illuminated sign on the gable: *"Be safe this Christmas"*. The word is they got it free from the brewery as their contribution to this year's anti-drink campaign.

But these sights were nothing compared with Batman's house. Carloads detoured from the Hecklescar road to take it in and others from the Great North Road would have done so had they known it was there. Uninhibited by any artistic ability and unrestrained by any woman, every Christmas Batman transforms his house into a winter palace of light. This year's theme is Harry Potter. A hardboard sheet panelled in purple and blood red, and studded with bulbs for nails has transformed the council front door into the gothic entrance of Hogwarts School for Wizards. Eerie stalagmites hang from the eaves; bats with red eyes hover from the clothes poles; an owl in dazzling yellow sits on an upstairs window sill and hoots when you clap your hands; a swollen green toad glows on the front step. All the windows are framed with lights flashing and twinkling and, if you listen carefully, playing Christmas pop songs. Glowing reindeer, labelled "Hagrid's Magical Creatures", gallop over the walls and light streamers squirm across the lawn masquerading as snakes wriggling round cauldrons and broomsticks. And the principals! What does it matter if Hermione resembles last year's Snow White in a black frock and Harry and Ron Weasley two of the Dwarfs in pointed hats? They are flamboyant, floodlit, and friendly; no one leaves without a smile and a donation to The Royal National Society for Deep Sea Fishermen.

Christmas touched the hearts of the people too; sparking excitement in the children, determination in the women and blind panic in the men as Santa letters were posted, secret presents were purchased and savings spent like confetti. Folk fretted about Christmas cards; the young hesitating over Mr and Mrs in case their friends had separated during the year and the old cautious about sending one at all in case theirs had died. And along the night streets and up and down the dark brae crept phantom postmen, stalking up paths, pushing those same cards through letter boxes and scuttling away to escape detection: cut out the Post Office; save stamps; do-it-yourself.

At Braeshiel, Christmas was welcomed with open arms. Although he would miss his father, John looked ahead to a fortnight of uplifting pleasure. His star had suddenly risen: glad tidings of great joy; Advent indeed. But Advent is also the time of reckoning - for our sins, not of commission only; of omission too: things left undone, truths not told - can we get away with those. Can he? He thought so. He bought a wreath and put it on the door; Morag brought him holly and he ordered a Christmas Tree from Delightful. (Do not enquire where he gets them.) When Mr Scott, his father's old friend, arrived on Sunday evening he entered into the season by asking for the Christmas mugs seeing as it was now Advent. He described them: Victorian street scenes, tall snowy houses, a snowy church and snowy trees and wrapped up Victorians trudging through snow beneath a starry snowy sky.

"Willie always took out them out for Advent and used them until the twelfth day. Silly old men!"

John could not recall having seen them but Mr Scott knew where there were kept - in the kitchen cupboard. At John's invitation the old minister hauled himself through to fetch them, but returned empty handed.

"Margaret!" exclaimed John and the following morning rang up his sister in Edinburgh.

"You haven't seen two Christmas mugs dad had, have you? Mr Scott said there were in the kitchen cupboard. Victorian snow scenes."

Had she seen them! She was looking at them as he talked; in the display cabinet of her art shop in Morningside labelled Bygone Christmases, price: £10.99 or £20 the pair.

"No, I can't say I have, but I'll look in the box Roddam brought from Braeshiel. We haven't had time to unpack all the stuff. If I find them do you want them back?"

"Yes," said John, "they seem to mean something to Mr Scott."

"You weren't thinking of giving him them, were you?" She sounded mildly alarmed.

"No," said John, "they'll stay at Braeshiel. If you find them send them on."

"I'll do that," she said, then added, but not to John, "No, I'm sorry, madam, the mugs are sold."

* * * * * * * * * * * * * * * * *

On Tuesday John went in high spirits to the School Christmas concert at the Village Hall. If ever an event captured the spirit of Christmas this is it. And we must all drink in the spirit of Christmas when we can for what else will sustain us through the dark days of winter. I would like to invite you to the next one, but there may not be a next one. The school roll is falling and those entrusted with the welfare of our children are contemplating removing them from the village. After Christmas they are taking away the infants' mistress, Mrs Douglas, veteran of 30 Christmases of concerts. So, who will produce next year's concert?

'*No whining you lot; what do villagers know about such important matters as demographics, education provision, resource management? Do they understand budgets? No, I thought not; they think it's just a matter of teaching the bairns to write, read and count and putting on concerts at Christmas.'*

You had better make sure you take it all in this year. Come to the long wooden hut next to the school. You will find yourself among friends. You will meet Helen and Alex, Delightful, Kit and Dod. Cecil from Surrey is here but not his wife; she's in a care home now, and there is Batman still making way with Lizzie Mitchell by the look of it; Jimmy Possum's just come in, and behind him Duncan and Sandy, Willie's old dominoes companions and behind them Bessie Collin with her niece. Dave Pallin of the Boy Peter, has run into Dot. I think she is telling him that he's late with his two dozen mince pies. Barbara with MS has just come in on two sticks with Malcolm her poor son and Peter her husband. Gloria is here to see her bairns perform and sitting next to her is Avril who has now left her husband to live with her accountant boyfriend in Hecklescar. Jessica, her daughter, lives with Avril's mother now so she can keep coming to Birsett school with her friends; she's the innkeeper's wife tonight. That's Rachel arrived now with Ben and Mr Scott has gone in beside her to keep her company. David is standing at the back with the other young fishermen, some of them young fathers. They won't sit down and will pretend the kid's stuff on the stage does not touch them. Morag and Calum are about somewhere. And there is Wanda peeking out from the kitchen door with Susan, who lost her son Johnny to the sea. They will be on tea duty later.

The concert this year, well, every year, is the Christmas story. We have had space men and animals tell it; this year it is the old story told from the point of view of "The Hoity-Toity Angel", an angel with attitude. She believes she is the "most stupendous angel in all the starry universe" and takes exception to singing for shepherds and babies in cattle troughs; she prefers Herod. However, in the end she gets her come-uppance (or rather come-downance) in the stable among dumb beasts and common folk. The old minister Mr Scott disapproves of this dumbing-down of the Christmas story, preferring the mystery of the old tale told in awe, but he is prepared to thole it if John, his ambitious executive friend, picks up the message of the treasure hid in common clay.

The lights go down and the children march down the aisle to squat at the front of the stage until it is their turn to take part. Mrs Douglas nods her head to Mrs Little on the piano, Mrs Little (Musical Director, peripatetic music teacher, wife of the gas man, pianist) sounds a note: the children stand and sing, "*O little town of Bethlehem*". In stilted actions and carefully learned speech, they lead us through the story, take us to Bethlehem, and introduce us to Gabriel, Joseph, Mary, Shepherds, three Wise Men, a nasty Herod and his henchmen, a galaxy of little stars and a host of angels. We can see that Torquil and Quentin are shepherds; Louise, our own heroine, is the eponymous Hoity-Toity Angel having given up the star role of Mary, the Mother of Jesus to Julie, Johnny's sister, even though she is just a beginner.

If we are willing, we can let the children lead us to see what they see with perfect clarity - the mystery of God come across all the universe and down through all ages to the village hall in Birsett. It would be ungrateful to resist them. They have practised for months to bring us the saving message and we are all in need of it. They have worked hard for your entertainment, do not deny them your pleasure. Closing song; full chorus and all principals: "*Good Christian Men rejoice*": women too; then switch the urn on for the tea.

Morag, by the way, although no longer a pupil has turned up as volunteer curtain drawer which partly explains why they jammed after the Herod scene and could not be used for the rest of the show.

The children take their curtain call bowing stiffly from the waist, as instructed, and grinning at their acclamation. Lady Flemington steps forward to say how jolly an evening we have all had and aren't the children jolly good and don't they deserve a jolly good round of applause. Then by a contrivance she steers her little speech towards decorating our homes for the Festive Season in a responsible manner and hints at an objection to villagers pillaging the holly trees up her drive. Morag who has been peeping from behind the curtain suddenly disappears behind it and John knows precisely where his holly came from.

In more generous mood Lady Flemington produces a bag full of sweet bars of various kinds and gives one to each child. She does this every year yet the children still make a fair show of being surprised. Then she announces mince pies and tea, and the doors to the back hall are flung open to reveal tables of them, plate upon plate of them, with Wanda, Susan, Dot, Spot and others waiting to serve. There's tea, coffee, orange juice for the bairns. We had better hurry or we'll end up with those big rock-like mince pies at the end; Wanda brought them. Go for those on the cake stand with the open tops, they're Dave Pallin's (the scone man), made to a secret recipe, makes the mincemeat himself. (If he was anything like as good a fisherman.....Shh, don't be like that, it's Christmas!)

The sparkling decorated hall fills with the clatter of cups, the banter and laughter of adults, the murmur of gossip and intrigue, and the skirling delight of children running, dancing, screaming. In the racket, the raffle is drawn and ten prizes are awarded. Helen wins the cake; she put it in. John, free of the anxieties that had plagued him and open to the spirit of season felt the warm comfort of the event, felt the affection, felt at home.

For a number of years, I was invited by the headmaster of Coldingham School to lead School Assembly. Here are two stories I told at Christma.

Gift of Kindness

There was once a young girl called Rachel. She was aged seven, and she lived in a village like Coldingham. She lived in an ordinary house next to a very big house in a big garden. In front of the house were large trees so you could hardly see the house when you walked past.

In the house there lived an old woman. Well, she wasn't that old, about 70, which isn't all that old, nowadays. This woman was called Mrs Grump. That's not her real name. In fact, no-one in the village knew her real name. She was called Mrs Grump because she was always grumpy. She had come to the village many years before and had bought the biggest house in the village because she was very rich and wanted everyone to know that she was very rich.

She had two children, who were now grown up; a boy, now a man, a very rich man, who lived in Switzerland, and a girl, now a woman, a very rich woman who lived in London. But they were so busy making money and being rich that they hardly ever visited Mrs Grump. That was one reason, I suppose, for her being grumpy.

No-body liked Mrs Grump, and you could understand why for she was very stuck-up and treated everyone as if they were peasants. Even the lady that went in to clean every day didn't like her. But Rachel felt sorry for Mrs Grump. She thought that perhaps she was lonely living in that big house all on her own.

So, when it came to Christmas, Rachel decided to do something about it. The Guides had decided to go round the

39

BRYAN WEBSTER

village a few days before Christmas Day singing carols, knocking at doors and asking people for money. They would send the money off to poor children in Africa.

When the carol singers came to the big house they were going to go straight past, but Rachel said,

'No, we will go to see Mrs Grump and, as she is very rich, she might give us a lot of money to send to the poor children.'

The others were not at all keen, but finally they agreed to go.

They walked through the gate and up the drive to the big front door. They rang the doorbell and started to sing "Good King Wenceslas", because, Rachel said, that it was about a very rich man helping the poor.. For a while nothing happened, so they rang the doorbell again, and carried on singing. When they had reached, '*Hither page come stand by me*', the door opened just a little, and Mrs Grump's face appeared in the space.

"Go away," she said, "I don't like carols."

"Could you give something for the children in Africa," piped up Rachel.

"No!" she said and slammed the door.

"There! We told you!" said the others to Rachel.

Rachel was very disappointed. But she had noticed something the others had not. She thought she had seen a tear in Mrs Grump's eye. Perhaps she was sad.

Rachel was quite right. Usually, one or other of her children, her son or her daughter, would make an effort to come to see her, or to take her to their own homes for a few days at Christmas. But this year her daughter was off to join her brother in Switzerland for a skiing holiday over Christmas, and would not be able to come to see her.

Of course, Rachel did not know this, but she had seen the tear in Mrs Grump's eye and it told her a lot. So, she was determined not to give up on Mrs Grump.

"Perhaps she doesn't have any presents". Rachel thought,

40

"I'll give her one."

But Rachel had no money and her mother would not give her any.

"You are not wasting money on that old grouch," she said, "she has plenty of her own."

At school, Rachel had been making a chain with paper strips. You know the kind of thing – loops of bright paper to hang up on the ceiling. She put it in a box, wrapped it up in Christmas paper and put a label on the outside: *"With love, from Rachel next door. Happy Christmas."*

On Christmas Eve, just as it was turning dark, she went to the big house, put her present on the step, rang the bell and ran away.

The following day, Christmas Day, quite early in the morning, there was a ring at the door of Rachel's house. Rachel's mother went to the door. There was Mrs Grump and in her hand she carried Rachel's little box.

"Does a girl called Rachel live here?" she said. She sounded very fierce.

Rachel's mummy said she did.

"Can I see her?" she demanded.

"Yes," said Rachel's mummy, "Come in."

Rachel had heard all this and trembled when she saw her parcel in Mrs Grump's hand.

Mrs Grump came in, sat down and asked Rachel.

"Did you leave this on my step?"

"Yes,"

Mrs Grump opened the present and took out the paper chain.

"And tell me, did you make this yourself?"

"Yes,"

Rachel's mummy butted in.

"Oh Rachel, how could you?"

"But I thought she might not have any presents!"

Mrs Grump replied, "No presents! I have many beautiful and expensive presents. My son has bought me a new car. My daughter has bought me a diamond necklace; and I have presents from all my relatives.

Rachel and her mother looked at the paper chain in Mrs Grump's hand. What was that beside all those expensive presents?

"But," said Mrs Grump, holding up Rachel's present, "this is my best present. For they just gave me money and gifts, you gave me your time, your kindness and yourself."

Then Mrs Grump took from her pocket a piece of paper.

"One good turn", she said, "deserves another. Here is a cheque for the African Children."

Rachel looked at the cheque. There was a one then three zeroes. A thousand pounds.!

"Now would you give me a hug for Christmas?"

Rachel gave her a big hug.

Christmas 2011

This Little Light of Mine

Last year when the schools broke up for Christmas a little girl called Lucy got off the school bus at the end of the lane that led to her home. Her father was a farmer and they lived on a high moor rather like Coldingham moor. They lived off the main road at the end of a short lane, about 100 yds. It was the only house for miles around. It was almost dark when Lucy reached home but Lucy was glad because she had made something at school she wanted to try out.

It was a lantern. Well, not a real lantern. They had taken a jam jar to school and painted it red and orange and yellow. Then tied a piece of wire round the neck to form a handle, then they took a candle and put it in the jam jar. When the candle was lit it shone out through the painted jar and looked just like a lantern.

Lucy was very pleased with her lantern and asked her mother if she could light it. Her mother was busy, so she said, 'later'. After half-an-hour she asked again and her mother said, 'later', then again and her mother said …….. 'later'.

Then her father came in and said to his wife and Lucy,

"It's blowing up a bad night out there, the snow has started to fall and the roads are beginning to get icy. The cars on the main road will need to watch what they are doing or they could end up in the ditch."

Lucy asked her father if she could light her lantern. And he said, "later."

They had their tea and after tea, as Lucy helped her mum with the washing up, she asked if she could light her lantern. And her mother said, ……

. No, not 'later'. She said, "What are you going to do with it once you have lit it?"

"Well," said Lucy, "I want to put it in the window."

"Whatever for?" said her mother.

"Well," said Lucy, "to show a light to people."

"What people?" asked her mother smiling, "There is no one here but us, no-one comes his way."

"Well, "said Lucy, "the teacher said that when Mary and Joseph and the baby Jesus were fleeing from Herod it was dark and they were lost and couldn't find anywhere to stay for the night. Then they saw a light in the window and were guided towards it. So, she said we should make lanterns and put them in the window in case there were strangers who were lost in the dark."

Her mother smiled and said, "Okay then, we'll light the candle, but not now, "later". After a while her father went out to see to the dogs, an,when he came back, said that the snow was piling up now And at last Lucy got to light her candle.

Out on the moor on the main road a car was moving very slowly because of the snow now covering the road. The road was very slippery. The car was being driven by a man and beside him sat his wife. In the back of the car was their young baby. They were coming home for Christmas. The man was driving very slowly because he could hardly see the road in front of him. Suddenly the car started sliding on the slippery snow. The man braked and that made things worse. The car slid ever so slowly off the road down a small bank and landed half on its side in a ditch. The man and woman and their baby weren't hurt and clambered out of the car as best they could. The snow swirled around them.

"We will need to get help," the woman said. "You'll need to ring the garage to come to tow us out."

"I haven't got your mobile phone," he said, "I thought you had it."

"No," she said, "I haven't got it. We'll have to find a house."

"There doesn't seem to be any houses around here," he replied.

"Just back there we passed a lane end. It might lead to a house."

"I'll go and see," said the man, "you stay here."

"No, you won't," said the woman, "We'll all go."

They set off and soon arrived at the lane end. They looked through the swirling snow, but could see nothing.

"I don't think it leads to a house," said the woman, beginning to panic at the thought of being out all alone on a night like this. The baby started to cry. And then they looked again and thought they saw . . ..

What do you think they saw?

Yes, they saw a light.

And where did the light come from?

Yes, from Lucy's lantern.

They were glad when they saw it. They went up to door, knocked and were let in to the warm fire.

Lucy's father got out the tractor and towed the car back onto the road and escorted them down to the village.

When he got back, Lucy had a question.

"Dad," she said. "it wasn't Mary and Joseph and the baby Jesus, was it?"

"Driving a Vauxhall Astra?" said her dad. "I don't think so, but they were strangers who were lost and saw your light."

THE KING AND THE TOYMAKER

This story I wrote with my great-neice Katie in mind. At the time I wrote it she was beginning to take part in the local pantomime.

At Christmas, we always see pictures of Santa Claus in his red coat delivering his toys by sleigh. Do you know why? I didn't until I asked. This is what I was told.

Once upon a time, in a country far away there lived a King who was very grumpy because he always got his own way. This was the fault of the courtiers who told him he could have anything he wanted.

"All you have to do," they said, "is to command it, and it will be done".

Then one day he went too far. He asked for something the courtiers couldn't give him. It made him grumpier than ever.

He had been visiting a neighbouring kingdom high in the mountains. The king there had sleigh and in the afternoon the two kings would ride along snow-covered forest tracks and through the villages and thoroughly enjoy themselves.

When our king came back to his own kingdom he commanded his courtiers to buy him a sleigh, the best one they could find.

The King was delighted with the sleigh they brought him. It was long, broad, beautiful and bouncy. There were four seats with cushions and blankets and plenty of room at the back for baggage.

"I can't wait to take a ride in it", cried the King, "hitch it to the horses, and bring it round to the front of the palace. I am going for a ride right away".

The courtiers looked at each other but none of them dared say what they were thinking which was, "he can't drive the sleigh for there is no snow". So, they carried the sleigh to the front of the palace and put the horses in the shafts. The King arrived all dressed up in his warm red robe trimmed with white fur, and walked down the stairs as to where the sleigh was waiting.

Now the King was no fool. He saw immediately that something was wrong.

"There is no snow!" he exclaimed. "I can't drive a sleigh when there's no snow!"

Then he turned to the courtiers in a rage.

"Get me some snow" he bellowed.

"Yes, your majesty," said the courtiers.

The King stamped back into the palace and went to sulk in his room.

The courtiers scurried off to the Weatherman.

"The King needs snow," they said, "please arrange it"

The Weatherman just laughed.

"I can't make it snow," he said, "I can only tell you if it is going to snow." He looked out of the window. "And it isn't."

The courtiers went to the King and told him what the Weatherman said. The King was furious.

"Lock the Weatherman up," he said, "and send for the Prime Minister."

When the Prime Minister arrived, the King told him that he wanted snow.

"But I can't make it snow, " said the Prime Minister.

"Do you want locked up?" shouted the King.

"No", replied the Prime Minister

"Then make it snow!", commanded the King.

The Prime Minister called together the parliament and after two days they passed an Act to make it snow the day after to-morrow.

However, when the day after to-morrow arrived, it didn't snow. In fact, the sun shone out of a clear blue sky. There was no sign of a snow cloud anywhere.

The King gave orders for the Prime Minister and all Members of Parliament to be locked up. Then he sent for the Chief Scientist.

"I have a scientific task for you," said the King. "Make it snow. If you do I will double your salary; if you don't I will have you locked up."

"But I can't make it snow," said the Chief Scientist.

"Lock him up," said the King to the courtiers, "and bring me the wisest men in all the kingdom".

When the wisest men heard what the King wanted and learned that the Weatherman, Prime Minister, Members of Parliament and Chief Scientist had all been locked up, they decided to leave the country. But the courtiers closed the borders and brought the wise men back to meet the King.

"I need your advice," said the King. "I need snow for my sleigh. Tell me how I can get it."

Now, of course, the wisest men did not know how to make it snow for the King, so they played for time.

"We'll need time to look into it," said the wise men.

"How much time?" asked the King.

"Three months, " they replied, hoping that before three months had passed it would have snowed anyway.

"Far too long," said the King. "I'll give you three days. Then if you cannot tell me how to make it snow, I will lock you all up."

When the wisest men left the King, they were very worried. They didn't know how to make it snow, but they didn't want the King to think they didn't know - and they didn't want to be locked up. However, as well as being wise, they were crafty.

"We'll find someone to blame," they said.

"I know," said the craftiest one of all, "we will blame the children, because they can't answer back. "

They all agreed that this was a very good idea.

They reported to the King that it was all the children's fault.

"How on earth can the children be to blame for there being no snow?" said the King.

"Well, " said the craftiest one, "in a few days it will be Christmas. The children want toys from the old toymaker in the far-off forest so they don't want it to snow in case the road to the toymaker becomes blocked. They are all wishing as hard as they can that it doesn't snow".

Now this wasn't true, the craftiest one of all had just made it up so the wise men would not be locked up.

It wasn't true, but the King believed them.

"The children, eh? " he roared. "Christmas, eh? Toys, eh? I'll teach them to meddle with the weather and with me. Christmas is banned!"

"Banned?" exclaimed the wisest men.

"Yes!" shouted the King

"Banned?" exclaimed the courtiers.

"Yes!" bellowed the King, "banned, banned, banned! Send horsemen to all parts of the kingdom to tell all children everywhere that Christmas is banned."

"He's gone too far this time," said the little Princess, his daughter, when she heard what he had done. She went to the king's room to see him. He had gone to bed in the sulks.

"Hallo, my precious. Have you come to cheer your father up? I am so depressed. There is no snow for my beautiful new sleigh and it's all the children's fault!"

"Poppycock!", cried the Princess.

"What?" said the King.

"Poppycock!" repeated his daughter, "Of course it's not the children. They have nothing to do with it. If it snows, it snows, if it doesn't, it doesn't. There is nothing anyone can do about it."

The King thought this might be true but he did not want to

admit it to a child.

"What do you know about it?" he said angrily, "You are just a child. Besides you are one of them. You are just trying to get me to change my mind. Well, I'm not. Christmas is banned, banned, banned!"

"Oh, please yourself," said the Princess, "but if Christmas is banned, you won't get any presents either. Not from me, and not from anyone else. It will serve you right for being so selfish and so grumpy."

This made the King even more depressed for he liked getting presents. But before he could say anymore, his daughter swung on her heel and walked out of the room.

In the far-off forest the old toymaker thought it strange that no children had come to see his toys. So, after a few days he set out on the long walk to the city where the King lived. As he passed through the villages on his way he was told, 'The King has banned Christmas'. But he didn't believe it; he couldn't believe it. No-one, not even a king, can ban Christmas. It just comes round year after year when the nights get longer and the winds get colder. It comes with the days and the weeks. No-one can ban it. But he was told over and over again, 'The King has banned Christmas'.

He made his way to the capital city. There he made enquiries and he asked the children why they had not come for their toys. 'The King has banned Christmas' they said.

"I must go and see the Princess" he said, "she will tell me the truth".

He went to the palace and asked to see the Princess.

Now the old toymaker did not know that through all his journey he had been watched by the king's spies and when he reached the palace they reported to the King that he had arrived.

"Arrest him and bring him before me. He is cause of all this trouble".

They brought the toymaker before the King.

"So, you are the trouble-maker!" shouted the King, without waiting to be introduced.

"Oh, no, your majesty", said the toymaker, "I'm just an old toymaker who lives in the far-off forest."

"No, you're not," ranted the King, "I know all about you. You and the children have stopped it snowing, and I need snow for my sleigh".

"But I can't stop it snowing if it wants to," said the toymaker, "neither can the children. "

"Well, I say you can, and I am the King!. I will give you until to-morrow to change your mind. If it is not snowing by 12 noon to-morrow, I will lock you up and I'll (the King was trying to think of nasty things to do to the toymaker) .... I'll destroy all your toys .... and I'll burn down your house....and I'll burn down the forest and I'll..."

The courtiers hurried the toymaker out of the king's presence before he could make any more threats. They were frightened that he was going to lock up all the people and burn the whole kingdom.

The toymaker walked sadly down the palace staircase. At the bottom he heard a voice from above.

"Hello", it said

He turned round. There was the little Princess. She came down to him.

"Aren't you the old toymaker?" she said.

"Yes," he replied.

"You look very sad. Is it something my father said?"

"Yes" said the toymaker and he told the Princess what the King had threatened.

"He's off his trolley", she said, "But I think I know a way to teach him a lesson".

The toymaker was so astonished that the Princess should speak in such a way about the King that he didn't say a thing. But we know that princesses can say anything they like about their fathers. They can't be locked up.

"This is what we'll do", went on the Princess, "we will get all the children of the city to tear up all the paper they have in their houses and bring them in bags to the palace to-morrow morning. I will take the bags up to the roof and at midday I will pour them down in front of the king's window. Then when the King looks out he will think it is snowing. He will let you go and you can escape to the forest before he finds out he has been tricked."

The old toymaker wasn't much taken with the plan but couldn't think of a better one. So, he thanked the little Princess, and went his way dreading the morrow.

The next day the old toymaker attended the palace with a heart as heavy as the clouds that now blocked out the sun. He didn't want his toys destroyed or his home burned or to be locked up, But he didn't like to trick the King either. He was sure no good would come of it. But he saw the little Princess on the stair and she told him to be brave.

"Well,", boomed the King, as the clock struck twelve, "Where is the snow?"

The toymaker replied as the Princess had taught him.

"Look out of the window, sire"

The King went to the window.

"Well," he repeated, "where is it.....just a minute, I thought I saw a flake.... there's another one. What big flakes. I do believe it's snowing. "

The old toymaker felt bad but was to feel a lot worse at what the King said next.

"Good," he said. "But I need enough snow for my sleigh. If I let you go, you will make it stop again. So go into the next room and come back in an hour. If it is still snowing then you may go home. Otherwise.........you know what will happen!"

The old toymaker trudged out of the room feeling more

miserable than ever. He thought of the poor little Princess pouring the paper from the roof, not knowing that all her efforts were in vain. Soon the paper would run out, the King would think it had stopped snowing and he would be back where he started. How he wished he was back in his little workshop in the forest. To make matters worse, there were no windows in the room he entered. He sat down beside the candle and wept.

The hour went by all too quickly and he trudged back into the king's room. The King was writing at his desk when he entered and for a few minutes he went on writing. The old toymaker avoided looking out of the window. He didn't want to see that the snow had stopped.

The King looked up.

"Now then," he said, "Now we will see". He got up and walked to the windows. The old toymaker closed his eyes and waited for the King to explode with anger.

What he heard next surprised him.

"Well done," said the King, "Well done, well done".

The toymaker looked at the King, then slowly looked out of the window. The snow was still falling. But how? The paper must have been used up long ago. He rushed to the window and stood beside the King. It was snowing, not paper snow, but snow snow. Down from sky it came in big white flakes, billowing and turning in the wind, swirling into the corners and out again, dancing and fluttering. The two men watched in wonder.

Everywhere they looked they could see snowflakes in their hundreds and thousands and their hundreds of thousands. The old toymaker looked down and through the falling curtain of flakes he could see that already the ground was covered. He opened his mouth but before he could speak, the door burst open and the little Princess danced into the room.

"It's snowing, it's snowing", she cried.

"Yes, my dear," aid the King, gently, "so it is. And I have been a foolish man not to listen to you. You said it would it would snow when it wanted to and you were right. You said no king could command it and you were right. It would not snow for me, but it snowed for the poor old toymaker."

He turned to the old man.

"I am very sorry, " he said.

"That's all right," said the toymaker, "but I need to get home now I have toys to make for Christmas." He paused.

"I suppose there will be Christmas now."

"Oh, yes, of course, of course. Send for the courtiers. Tell them to send horsemen through the land to tell everyone that Christmas is unbanned. And let the Weatherman, the Prime Minister, the Members of Parliament, and Chief Scientist go free."

"But what about the wisest men?" said the Princess, "they blamed the children!"

"Oh, them," said the King, "lock them all up".

"Oh, no, not again" sighed the little Princess, "I know what - make them shovel snow to clear the pavements for the poor people."

"What a good idea, " said the King, "It is so decreed".

But our story is not quite over. The old toymaker returned to his workshop in the far-off forest to finish making his toys. With all the fuss he had been kept late and it was Christmas Eve before he finished. When all the toys were ready he looked out of his door to discover that the road was blocked so the children would not be able to collect their toys. Whilst he was standing at his door wondering what he could do, he heard the jingle of sleigh bells and over the rising ground he saw a sleigh drawn by six reindeer approaching. He recognised the driver immediately. Only the King had a red coat trimmed with white fur. The King drew up. Beside him was the little Princess.

"The Princess said you'd be snowed up and the children would not be able to come to you" said the King, "So I have come to offer to deliver them for you. It gives me the chance to do something useful for a change. After all, it is my fault everything's so late."

The old toymaker agreed at once and the toys were loaded onto the sleigh. Then the King and the Princess rode away to deliver the toys in the villages, towns and city.

It was dark by the time they reached the houses and children heard first the jingle of the sleigh bells in the street outside. Then, looking out, they saw the sleigh go by driven by the King who (as we know) was dressed in his magnificent red coat with white fur at the cuffs and the collar. And on Christmas Day they found their toys lying at the foot of their beds.

That is why Santa Clause is always shown wearing a red coat trimmed with white fur driving a sleigh through the snowy skies.

Christmas 2001

WHAT CAN I GIVE HIM?

Mary Webste

My Mary wrote this story about putting on a school play at Christmas. She had done it many times.

Alan Mackay looked at the porridge in his plate and glowered. Still glowering, he lifted the milk jug and with studied care, poured the creamy milk round the grey circle of porridge.

'Alan!' His mother's voice from the doorway made him start.

'Ye ken this is the morning I go tae the big hoose. Get that porridge eaten. Hurry up now. Ye'll be late for the school.'

Slowly Alan supped the porridge, his gloom deepening with each spoon. He'd had a week's holiday from school, and for the few blissful autumn days, he'd run free on the hills round the farm. The thought of school was more than his six years could bear. He looked at Jess, the collie, lying in front of the fire and the collie looked soulfully back at him. Alan gulped down the last spoonful of porridge, swung his legs down from the chair, and trailing his school bag by the strap from beside the fire, he made reluctantly for the door.

'Hev ye yer dinner money, Alan?' he heard his mother call.

'Aye,' shouted Alan back over his shoulder.

'Hev ye a hankie?'

'Aye.'

Without turning round, he held up a grimy handkerchief for her to see, then with a sudden spurt of energy, he ran down the farm track that led from his home, his despair forgotten in the brightness of the November morning.

The sight of Miss Munro putting her bike away in the school shed brought him to a halt and his spirits sank again. Then, from behind him came a rush of feet, and without turning round he knew who it would be. It was Fiona, her fair pony tail bobbing behind her and her eyes dancing with excitement.

'Alan,' she panted, 'I went to Edinburgh on Saturday.'

Alan eyed her coldly and quickened his step.

Not in the least disconcerted, Fiona chattered on.

'I've seen the doll I'm getting for Christmas. Christmas is only eight weeks and three days away. I counted it on the calendar.'

Alan showed no interest but his spirits lifted. Christmas! He'd forgotten about Christmas. Maybe he'd get a bike. . . or an Action Man... or a garage, or . . .. Even school was different. There were decorations and parties and games. And, of course, the School Play! They would all get dressed up. There would be Mary and Joseph and the shepherds, and oh! The Kings! How he'd envied the Kings last year, with their ermine-trimmed robes, their shining gold crowns and their precious, mysterious gifts. Oh, to be a King! To wear a glittering crown! He caught his breath at the wonderful possibility. His heart soared.

'I'll race you to the gate,' he shouted to Fiona, and, when she caught up with him, he banged her with his bag just to show he liked her. They ran together to the school door.

The morning prayer was over and the children sat down with much shuffling and sniffing and coughing.

'Well,' said Miss Munro, 'Have you all had a good holiday?'

'Yes, Miss,' the children chorused back.

'Has anyone anything to tells us?' asked Miss Munro.

Fiona had.

'Miss Munro, I've been to Edinburgh and I've seen the doll I'm going to get for Christmas.'

One by one the children told of their outings and doings. Alan sat racking his brains for something to tell. Suddenly his hand shot up.

'Please, Miss, Jess is going to have pups.'

Some of the older girls tittered and Alan wished he'd said nothing. His face and neck blushed a fiery red. To ease his embarrassment, Miss Munro said quickly,

'That's lovely, Alan. Maybe your dad will let you keep one

and you can bring it to the school for us all to see.'

Vindicated, Alan turned to the girls and made a face at them.

When he turned back Miss Munro was at the piano.

'We'll start learning our Christmas Carols today,' she said, 'Christmas isn't so far away.'

'Just eight weeks and three days,' piped up Fiona, 'I counted on my calendar.'

'Yes, Fiona, that's right. So, we'll have to start thinking about our play too. I'll choose the people for it tomorrow.'

A vision of the Kings in their golden splendour glowed in Alan's mind. He sang the carols with fervour. Then sums, reading, writing, gym, handwork – the day wandered on through the haze of Alan's dreams – dreams of gifts, and crowns and fur-trimmed robes.

Next day, he was up and ready for school before his father left for work. By half-past eight he was at school, hovering around the small huddle of boys who clustered round the school gate, arguing noisily about their favourite football teams. Alan thought Miss Munro would never come, but at last he saw her bike coming over the hill. As she reached the gate, Alan opened it for her, and while she put her bike away, carried her bag into the classroom. She took it from him with a smile, a special smile, Alan thought, a smile that promised his dreams would come true. He closed the door behind him with exaggerated care, then whooped as he ran down the playground to join in the argumentative game of football the others had started.

Alan was in his chair before the bell stopped ringing sitting up with arms folded and face aglow. Miss Munro looked at Alan and smiled. She liked Alan. He was the youngest in the second class, small for his age and sensitive. She often found herself protecting him from the harshness of the older children. Now he was trying to impress her and she wondered why.

Alan blurted it out.

'Are we starting the play to-day, Miss?'

So that was it!

'Yes, Alan. We'll choose the people this morning.'

'Hurry up', Alan whispered as the children passed his desk. 'Hurry up! We're doing the play today.'

Oh, that dinner money and register. Would they never get started!

But at last Miss Munro took a notebook from her bag.

'I've chosen the people for our play', she announced to the children.

A tingling excitement welled up inside Alan.

'Fiona, I want you to be Mary. John you'll be Joseph and William will be the innkeeper. Annette and Sheila and the girls in Primary One will be angels.

Miss Munro went on concentrating on her notebook.

'Alan!'

Alan's heart was a bursting point.

'Alan, you are going to be a shepherd and the boys in Primary One will be shepherds too.'

A shepherd! Alan could not take it in. It could not be. But the teacher went on. She was talking about the Kings.

'Ian. . ... Dugard . . . . . .Tommy will be the Kings.'

Miss Munro looked up, checking that no-one had been forgotten and, as she did, her gaze rested on Alan. He sat there, the tingling excitement draining into numb disappointment.

His eyes pleaded. 'Please Miss,' he said, 'I was a shepherd last year.'

Miss Munro understood him at once. So that's what he'd wanted - to be a King. But there was nothing she could do. The three boys in the top class were the obvious choice. She collected her thoughts desperately.

'I know you were a shepherd last year,' she said, 'But you see, Alan, I want you to be leader of the shepherds. . . the one who gives the lamb to Jesus . . . After all, your dad is a shepherd so you'll know all about it.'

She had done her best. Quickly she changed the subject.

'Right then, children. Move back your desks and we'll make the stable.'

The children obeyed with noisy enthusiasm.

'Please, Miss, Alan's crying,' said Fiona.

Miss Munro went up to his desk and knelt beside him.

She put her arm round his sobbing shoulders and said,
'What's wrong, Alan?'

There was no answer.

'Come on,' she said coaxingly, 'I can't do without my chief
shepherd.'

'Please, Miss, I have a sore head.'

'I thought you didn't look well this morning,' she lied and
left him his pride. 'Come and stand beside me.'

She led him to her desk and, with her arm still round him,
began to rehearse the play.

For a while, Alan stood sobbing. Then lifting his head, he
brushed back his tears, leaving grey, muddy streaks all down his
face.

'Miss Munro, I feel better now,' he said, and she sent him to
join the other shepherds.

'Make room for your leader, shepherds,' she called. 'Take this
pointer for your crook today, Alan. We'll get a real one for the
play . . .. and we'll have to remember to get you a lamb.'

In the following weeks the excitement grew. Every morning
villagers passing to the shop, could hear the cheery sound of carols
coming from the school. Inside the classroom was bright with
decorations, glittering calendars, lanterns and painted fir-cones.
More and more time in the school was given over to the play.

Alan was beginning to enjoy his part.

'Please miss I should have a dug,' he said one day. 'Ye canna
be a shepherd without a dug,' he protested to his subordinate
shepherds. The children sniggered.

'I suppose you'll be wanting real sheep next,' said Miss
Munro and the room exploded with the children's laughter.

The week before Christmas, cloaks and dresses carefully
stored away the year before, were taken from the cupboard and
the children fitted out. Alan felt quite pleased with himself in
his striped green and yellow cloak. A white towel was tied

precariously on his head and, in his hand, he carried a crook that his father had made for him. At the very bottom of the box lay the gold, frankincense and myrrh. What did it matter if the rest of the world saw a fancy box and bottles gilded and painted? To the children they were the priceless treasures of the Kings. Miss Munro laid them on her desk and the children fingered them wonderingly. The Kings made their crowns and sprayed them, two gold and one silver. Once the gilt had dried, the crowns were stuck round with fruit-gums. But as they varnished them the children did not see fruit-gums. They saw emeralds, rubies and amethysts. Then with loving care the crowns were placed with loving care on top of the piano beside the gold, frankincense and myrrh.

'Please Miss, please Miss,' Alan hopped around his harassed teacher with his hand up.

'What is it, Alan?' Miss Munro turned to him.

'Please, Miss Munro, what can I give him?'

'Oh, yes, Alan,' Miss Munro put up a hand to her aching head. 'I must remember to bring the lamb tomorrow.'

Alan met her at the gate the next morning. The 'lamb', wrapped in brown paper was in the bike basket. Alan ran to the classroom with it. He tore off the brown paper. His eyes fell.

'Aw Miss,' he said, 'It's mair like a poodle than a lamb.'

'No, it isn't' answered Miss Munro absent-mindedly, for she was sorting the angels' wings. Alan squinted at the stuffed toy through half-closed eyes trying to see it like a lamb, but it still looked like a poodle.

'But please, Miss,' he started again.

'Alan,' mumbled Miss Munro through a mouthful of safety pins. 'It will have to do.'

The afternoon of the play came. On the rows of chairs set out in the headmaster's classroom, sat the mothers, chatting and smiling, almost as nervous as their children. From next door they could hear the children's voices.

'Where's the myrrh? I've lost the myrrh.'

'Oh dear, my headdress is falling off.'

And, more belligerent, from an angel,

'Watch ma wings.'

Miss Munro hushed the children.

'Miss Munro, I need to go to the toilet.'

It was Alan's voice.

'Poor Alan,' thought Miss Munro, 'He's spent all day in the toilet.'

With final instructions and a prayer that all would go well, Miss Munro went out to face the audience and sat down at the piano. The chatter subsided. She nodded to the headmaster. He stood up and welcomed the mothers and the play began.

One by one the children made their appearance – Mary, Joseph, the inn-keeper, the angels, and everyone was caught up once more in the wonder of the Christmas story. Then it was time for the shepherds. Miss Munro played the boisterous tune that heralded the shepherds' entrance. There was no movement from the classroom door. She turned towards it.

'The shepherds,' she hissed.

'Alan's away to the toilet,' came the whispered reply.

Miss Munro started again and played the tune through as slowly as she could. Then, to her relief, she saw Alan pushing his way to the front of the shepherds. In gratitude she closed her eyes as the shepherds shuffled their way to the manger. Quiet laughter rippled through the audience. Miss Munro, behind the piano, wondered what the shepherds were up to. But all was well. She heard Alan's high-pitched voice begin.

'We are only poor people. We have so little we can bring but we wanted to bring something to the Baby, so we have brought Him a wee pup.'

A wee pup! The words slapped into Miss Munro's mind. She peered round the piano. Round the manger knelt the shepherds, their faces alight. Fiona, a radiant Madonna was smiling at Alan. Yes, there was Alan. By his side was Jess, the collie, and in his outstretched hands was a pup. Jess nuzzled the black and white wriggling bundle and whined.

'Sit, Jess,' Alan whispered and the collie obediently lay down at Alan's feet. Then he laid the pup beside her and it snuggled contently into the collie's side.

How the rest of the play got by, Miss Munro never knew. But from the applause she could tell the end had been reached. Thankfully, she retreated with the children into her classroom.

'Alan,' her voice was accusing. 'Where's the lamb?'

'Please Miss, Jesus wouldn't have liked it. He'll like the dug, though. He'll have grand fun with a dug.'

Miss Munro looked at the earnest face and smiled. She could not but agree.

c.1970
Christmas 2019

THIRD DONKEY (NON-SPEAKING)

His 47 years had dwindled to a beer belly and a game of darts on a Friday night. If he could get one of the women drunk enough not to be too choosy, there might be a little something afterwards. Then there was the boy.

His days, Monday to Friday he spent at Dorkings, the builders' merchants, driving a fork lift truck, ferrying pallets off lorries into the warehouse; lifting pallets from the warehouse into vans. He hated the job; hated Ferguson, the foreman, and skived so much that his workmates despised him. 'Fat slob' was the least bad of the titles by which he was known. The job gave him a wage, a pathetic wage, £1.50 above the minimum rate; that's all.

'Not enough for a piss up' he complained.

He meant it to be funny, but he had squeezed the humour out of his life; now his jokes limped out as bitter whines.

Of course there was more, there was the boy - and the house. A council house on the Mardon Estate; in the rundown, litter-strewn part of the estate; the part that no one who didn't live there ever visited; certainly not at night. The house had to be looked after. He resented looking after the house.

Before Genista left he had done nothing in the house; now he was expected to do it all. And she'd left him with the boy, her boy. His too, of course, but she should have taken him with her when she went off with her fancy man to Scunthorpe. That's what mothers are for. But she didn't want him.

So, as well as the job and the house, he has to look after the boy. The house is a tip. He runs the hoover round occasionally, and keeps his greasy armchair clear of debris so he can slump in it to watch TV. The TV! Never off! It goes on in the morning and stays on all day; he falls asleep in front of it most nights and only wakes to go to bed. Sometimes he remembers to switch it off when he goes to work, or the boy does it when he leaves for school. The boy gets his own breakfast: Weetabix with milk, if there is any milk; if not, not - if there's Weetabix.

As a Primary Five from a deprived area, the boy gets free school meals and eats crisps at night – in his own room that he tries to keep clean and tidy. Auntie Maggie buys his clothes, and is sometimes refunded. She washes the boy's clothes, making sure her brother has not sneaked his own into the pile. If she started washing his clothes as well, it would just encourage him to be lazier than he is now. She comes on a Friday evening when he is out. Sometimes, when he stays out all night, the boy, frightened, rings her up and she takes him home. But her husband objects. 'Where's his father?' he says, 'or his mother, for that matter?'

In late November, the boy brought home a note from the school. Addressed to the parents, parent or guardian, it requested permission for:

'the below mentioned pupil is to take part in the School Nativity Play which is based on the story of the birth of Jesus, and thus has some Christian religious content which some parents may find inappropriate to their own beliefs:'

Kevin McBride: Third Donkey (non-speaking).

The boy said he wanted to be in the play, so he signed the slip, and the boy took it back to school the following day.

On the Friday of the first week in December, the boy arrived home with a donkey outfit; a brown furry jump suit and a donkey face mask. He said that Mrs Golightly had said that his father had to wash the outfit, both parts, and return it to the school by Monday.

'The hell I will.' said the father, before he left for darts at the club.

The boy put the jumpsuit and the face mask in the washing machine with some powder and switched it on. The suit came out crushed and creased. One of the sets of eyelashes on the mask came adrift and the boy found it lying in the bottom of the machine. Scared of what the teacher might say, he phoned Aunt Maggie, who on Sunday night came round and sewed the eyelashes back on again.

Mrs Golightly said the jump suit was a disgrace and, when he admitted that he had washed it himself, started to give the boy orders to take it back to his mother to do it properly. At that the boy had dissolved into tears, and had to explain to Mrs Golightly what his class teacher already knew - that he never saw his mother and that she did nothing for him. Mrs Golightly took the jump suit home and washed it herself.

'Cannot do it,' he said when the boy bought home an invitation to the Nativity Play, 'They've picked the wrong night. It's darts on a Friday night. And it's the Christmas Special. I couldn't miss that. Did'ye not tell them it's your father's darts night. You know I play darts on a Friday. It's the only night I get out. Give it to your Aunt Maggie. She'll go'

Aunt Maggie came on the phone.

'I can't go; it's the office party. You'll have to take him.'

'I can't.'

'But he's in it. All the other kids will have their parents there. He'll be disappointed if you don't go.'

'Disappointed! Not half as f***** disappointed as me if I don't get to the darts. It's the Christmas Special. And, by the by, he'll need to sleep at your place. I won't be back till late.'

'But he's got a part in it. He's that pleased he's got a part. He wanted you to see him in it.'

'Yes, three cheers for the f****** third donkey – non-speaking. D'ye think I'm going to miss the darts for a third donkey? I work bloody hard. I deserve a bit of relaxation.'

'Well, I can't take him. But if you bring him round here later. He can stay here the night.'

'Ye're not listening Maggie. I won't be f***** here. He'll come on his own. He knows the way.'

Maggie spat back.

'You're a nasty man, my brother, a nasty man. Poor Kevin

saddled with a father like you.'

Maggie slammed down the phone.

'There'll be plenty people there anyway', she comforted herself, 'to see him. It's not that far to the school and back here. There'll be plenty of people around. I'll tell him to come straight here afterwards. He'll be alright.'

Mrs Golightly had said that they had to be there at half past six at the latest. At the latest! So, on a dark cold December night, the boy set out from his house at quarter past six. He let himself out; his father was having a shower in preparation of his night out at the Christmas Special.

'Maggie's not going to spoil my night out,' he grumbled as made his way to the Black Swan. 'It's not much to ask. Third donkey – non speaking! How important is that?'

He was amongst the first to arrive at The Black Swan and went straight to the bar to buy himself a drink. Mike came in shortly afterwards and joined him.

'I'm surprised to see you here so early,' said Mike. 'I thought you'd be going to the play thing at the school. The wife's away to it. You have a little laddie at the school, don't you? He's a donkey or something I think Barbara said?'

'Is he now? I didn't want to miss the draw for the darts. I feel I'm on form tonight.'

'The draw's not till eight – or whenever they get started. You could have come in later. That's what the wife's doing. She's coming in later. You could have. . .. '

'But I didn't, did I! Why is everyone f****** lecturing me. They should try bringing up a kid on their own. I didn't ask to be stuck with him. Anyway, he's not on his own; Maggie's taking him. It's a woman's job - and I don't have a woman. Right? At least not yet. But who knows?'

He leered and laughed. Mike smiled and walked away.

Then a woman arrived. Rita, not a favourite, but a woman nonetheless.

'We're having a bit of fun through in the snug before the

serious darts start. Are you game?'

'You know me, darling, lead me to it.'

Marvin was in charge. He explained the first game. They all had to throw three darts. Whoever got the lowest score had to pay a penalty nominated by the one that scored the highest. There were four of them. Rita threw first: 87, then Marvin: 75; decent scores, but he thought he could match them. In any case it was Bertha to throw next: Barn Door Bertha (as in 'couldn't hit'): Two treble twenties and an 18: 138. His turn: treble twenty, 10, treble 1: 73. Lowest score.

'The Donkey's Tail,' Bertha announced.

'Donkey's Tail! Donkey! The word smacked into him, followed immediately by four others: 'Third Donkey (non-speaking)'.

He heard Maggie's voice in his head: 'You're a nasty man, my brother. Poor Kevin saddled with a father like you.'

He struggled to shut his ears to it.

In a haze he was shown the picture of a donkey stuck on the wall. It had no tail. He was to be blindfolded and the tail placed in his hand. He had to pin the tail to the donkey. With a trembling hand he took the tail from Bertha.'

'He's got the shakes,' she yelled and the others laughed. As the tail was placed in his hand, Mike walked in. In the darkness of the blindfold, he heard Mike say to the laughs of the others,

'The revenge of the donkeys. His lad's a donkey at the school.'

Suddenly he threw down the tail and stripped off the blindfold. Without speaking he strode out of the snug, out of the bar, out of The Black Swan, into the winter's night. Out! He wanted out, he wanted away, but away from what? A donkey without a tail, or a donkey (non-speaking)? The two coalesced in his mind – and his conscience, or should it be his concern. A concern that had long been locked up in his resentment. Resentment at what? At the job, the house, the meals, the shopping, the pay, the humdrum, drumming, humming of life, bored and pissed off. It was not his fault. He did not deserve it. Genista walked out – and left the boy with me. The boy! His resentment had boiled and distilled and settled on the boy. Third donkey (non-speaking). You're not important! Shut up! You have nothing to say! Bottom of the pile! Like his ......like his.....father. His father! Like me! But I am his father!

Suddenly, surprisingly, he found himself outside the school. By what steps he had arrived there he did not know, but there was the school; the school bright with Christmas, and his son in it, in the play, and wanted his father to see him. That was all; just to sit and watch and be there for him. But he'll be too late, won't he?

Yes, he is too late. He has missed the play. The children are taking their bows when he walks in. There are no seats at the back, so he is motioned to a seat at the front. He sits down and joins in the applause.

'And now for the wonderful donkeys,' Mrs Golightly announces. 'Take your heads off children.'

Kevin's anxious eyes emerge from the donkey's head. Then he catches sight of his father. His face breaks into a beaming smile and he raises a hoof to wave to his father. His father stands up and shouts, 'I'm here, son.' The audience laughs out loud and cheers.

'He did splendidly, did he not?' said Mrs Golightly to the father when Kevin introduced them over the ginger wine and mince pies.

'Yes,' he said, 'he did. Best in the show!'

When Kevin had divested himself of his donkey suit, and said goodbye to Mrs Golightly, his father put his arm round his shoulder and said to him.

'We'll nip to the chip shop and get a bag to take home, eh?'

'But are you not going to the darts?'

'Naw,' said his father, 'not tonight, son.'

Christmas 2017

CHRISTMAS TREES AND CANDLES

This story is a refugee from another collection of mine, 'Eyemouth and the Hecklescar Stories'. Like the others, I had sketched it out many years ago, but had not finished it before that collection was published.

I f you had been standing on the pier-end in Hecklescar at nine o'clock on that Saturday, the second before Christmas, you would have seen the seine-netter Cornucopia leave the harbour and head north into a choppy sea. And, if you knew the ways of Hecklescar fishermen, you would have wondered why.

On every other day of the week, except Sunday, there would be nothing strange about a fishing boat heading out to sea, but on Saturday they stayed at home. Saturday is for repairing the damage from last week's fishing and preparing for the week to come. It is a time to stand on the pier and talk about the size of catches, the price of small whitings, and the stupidity of the White Fish Authority. It is not a time for putting out to sea.

You would, therefore, have asked why the Cornucopia was setting out – and, if you were in the know, your question would have led you to Candles, one of the town's refuse collectors. His occupation, however, has nothing to do with this story. It merely explains how Charles and Tam, the other two members of the refuse collection crew, came to be on board the Cornucopia that morning.

Each year, Candles arranged a somewhat suspect deal with a forester on the Cocklaw Estate whereby the forester provided Candles with Christmas Trees at a price well below what the estate would have received on the open market; Candles collected them and sold them.

In case you think there is something dodgy, nay, unChristmaslike, about this transaction let me point you to the parish minister of Hecklescar, the Rev John McFarlane. He always orders a tree from Candles, the biggest one, in fact – for the kirk. If any of his sniffier elders run into Candles and cast doubt upon the transaction, Candles will tell them what the minister says to him,

'Trees belong to no man. We may plant them, but God giveth the increase.'

This year, however, a problem had arisen over the transportation of the trees. Last year, Candles had paid Johnny Traction £10 for the task, but this year Johnny had doubled the price and Candles had refused to pay. In a moment of entrepreneurial inspiration, Candles had hit on the solution: transport them by sea. This fulfilled two long felt needs for Candles: it gave him less expense and would score a long-sought victory over Traction.

Incidentally, you will probably have gathered that Traction is not Johnny's family name. Family names are not much use in Hecklescar where most families share the few surnames available. Johnny was named Traction because he owned the only general transport business in the town. Put it another way – he drove the only lorry not dedicated to fish.

Candles had hired the Cornucopia, its crew and skipper, Spotless, to collect the trees. That is why on that Saturday the Cornucopia left the harbour and headed up the coast to the little port of Cockshaven.

In spite of the choppy conditions the boat reached Cockshaven in three-quarters an hour. There, they met the furtive forester with his trailer load of trees. As soon as the boat tied up Charles climbed onto the trailer and threw a tree onto the boat's deck. Spotless picked it up by its tip as he would a dead rat by its tail.

"And whit dae ye think ye're daein'?" he shouted to Charles. "Ye're droppin' pine needles a' ower the boat."

He was not called 'Spotless' for nothing. It was said in Hecklescar that a decent catch of fish disheartened him, because he got nasty, smelly fish scales all over his nice clean deck. He had anticipated that Christmas trees would be a cleaner cargo.

Candles stepped from the galley to mediate.

"Whit's the matter?" he asked.

"Ye'll hev tae be mair careful with thae trees," replied Spotless.

"Sorry," said Candles and turned to Charles who was standing on the trailer with the next tree in hand poised for flight.

"Mind the man's boat," shouted Candles. "We dinna' want tae get it a' dirty after the man's jist cleaned it."

He smiled at Spotless who, reassured, gently laid the delinquent tree on the deck. Candles winked at Charles then clambered forward to the hatches.

"Right then," he said to Spotless, "you and Tam go down below and I'll hand the trees down to you through the hatch."

Spotless was horrified.

"Ye're no thinkin' o' pittin' thae things doon ma hold, are ye?"

"Well, aye...."

"No way! Ye're not on!"

"Whit fer no? They're a' guid clean trees, jist chopped."

"Ye're not pittin' ony trees doon ma hold. It's for fish, not trees!"

"Well, it's gey little used," snapped Candles, then immediately regretted it.

Spotless glowered at him a moment or tw, then stomped into the wheelhouse and started the engine. He pulled down the window and shouted to the crewman standing in the bow.

"Let go for'ard!"

The man leapt ashore and went to the iron rung that held the mooring rope.

Candles dropped his shoulders and approached the wheelhouse window.

"A'right, a'right," he conceded, "we'll leave them on the deck."

Spotless stopped the engine.

The trees were lowered one by one onto the deck where Candles and Tam stacked them row on row. By the time they were finished the trees covered the foredeck and were stacked three or four deep aft of the wheelhouse.

Loading complete, the boat gingerly left the pier and nosed out into the bay, resembling nothing so much as a floating hedgehog.

Once clear of the breakwater, Candles felt the boat heave in the gathering swell and began to suspect that the shipping trade has its drawbacks. The further out they headed the more the boat pitched and dived.

"Tree overboard!" came a laughing shout from the stern.

Candles staggered aft to see one of his trees wallowing in the boat's wake. As he watched, another toppled into the sea to join it. A wave broke over the bow and the trees propped on the starboard gunwale shifted uneasily.

Tam rolled forward to push them back into place. While he was busy, two from the port side toppled over the side, but their topmost branches tangled with the other trees and hung poised over the sea. Charles, on his way through the forest to free them, tripped and shook them free. Candles watched helplessly as they floated away.

"Keep an eye on thae trees," shouted Spotless from the wheelhouse. "They're liftin' the paint on the gunwales."

Candles' reply was taken away with the wind, which, from his expression was just as well. Another shout from the stern told him that more trees had taken to the water. Thus, they battled on along the coast, with the three men staggering back and forwards trying to protect their cargo, Spotless in the wheelhouse grumbling about the mess, and the crew keeping a running tally of the number of trees that had fallen overboard. It was the hardest day's work that Candles had put in for a long time and he was exhausted when the Cornucopia slid into the quiet waters of Hecklescar harbour.

By the following Saturday, however, the trials of the boat trip had faded. Candles had recovered his bounce and whilst he and Tam delivered trees in Hecklescar, Charles was despatched to The Shore, a little fishing village a few miles up the coast. Charles belonged to The Shore, and, having a relative in every second house, expected sales to be brisk.

In an hour and a half of exceptional energy and unusual pleasantness, Candles and Tam delivered their load and retreated to The Basking Shark to await Charles. While Tam supped a well-earned pint, Candles counted the takings. The clock above the bar ticked off half-an-hour.

"Where's the man got tae?" grumbled Candles.

"He'll be takin' a drink o' tea wi' a' his relatives," said Tam. "They hev an awfu' thirst for tea, that crowd. Ye would think they had shares in a plantation the way they slop it oot and pour it doon."

The clock ticked on. Candles ordered another drink. Thirty more minutes passed. Finally, Candles' frustration boiled over. He leapt to his feet and stomped to the door. Tam drained his glass then followed him. He pushed open the door and ran into Candles who had stopped abruptly in the passage.

"Look at the man," hissed Candles, and pointed to a hunched figure walking back and forwards in front of the pub's lighted windows. Charles was clearly making up a story. His mouth moved as he rehearsed his speech. He seemed satisfied and moved towards the door, then stopped, shook his head, turned back and started his speech-making again. Candles voice shattered his concentration.

"And where dae ye think ye've been?"

Charles froze in the middle of one of his gestures, then slowly turned to face Candles.

"I could dae wi' a drink," he said.

Candles ushered him into the pub and bought three half-pints. He put one down in front of Charles.

"Now then," demanded Candles, "Where hev ye been?"

Charles took a long swallow of extra heavy and blurted out the answer.

"I've been up tae Buttermains, an' Billiedean, and a' the ferms, an' halfway tae Berwick, but naebody wants Christmas trees."

"Whit hev ye been trekkin' roond the country fer. Thae trees were fer yer relatives at The Shore. Whit aboot them?"

"They a' hev them!"

"They hev them!" exploded Candles, "Whit dae ye mean, they hev them?"

"Well," mumbled Charles, they got them off......." He stopped, took a drink, then spat out the name. "They got them off Johnny Traction!"

"Johnny Traction! Johnny Traction!" roared Candles.

The crisis over, Charles became talkative.

"He's been deliverin' them a' week, an' he's only been takin' five pence a foot, and he's had them treated....."

Candles had heard enough.

"Five pence a foot – that's less than I paid for them!"

"An' they've been treated," repeated Charles.

"Ye canna' get them for five pence a foot – anywhere. I ken, I've tried. Ye canna' buy them for that!"

Charles tried again. "An' they've been treated."

Tam took an interest in the treatment.

"Whit dae ye mean – 'treated'?"

"It's a special mixture," explained Charles. "It stops the pine needles frae droppin' on the carpet. Cousin Billy says his tree was drippin' wi' the stuff when Traction brought it."

Candles still struggled with the economics.

"I tried everywhere. Ye canna' get them for less than eight pence a foot, so how can he charge five pence and make anything off them?"

Tam tried to help.

"Maybe he's tryin' to capture the market."

"And whit's the point of capturin' the market, if ye no' mak' anything off it?" Candles demanded.

The force of the argument silenced Tam. Charles remained impressed by the mixture.

"That wis his ace card," he said. "Traction must ken that when a man buys a Christmas tree, his peace of mind depends on no' getting' pine needles a' ower the carpet."

As he spoke, the door opened and in walked the man himself with a grin the length of Leith Walk. He walked up to the counter and ordered himself a large whisky. Then he waved his hand towards Candles and his two companions.

"An' gie ane tae the lads frae me. They dae a grand job keepin' the toon clean and tidy."

The barman put down the glasses in front of the three men

"Here's tae ye," proposed Traction, raising his glass.

"Where did ye get them?" growled Candles.

"Get what?" asked Johnny Traction, innocently.

"The trees, that's whit! Where did ye get them?"

Traction supped his drink thoughtfully.

"Weel," he said slowly, "it's no for a businessman tae disclose his suppliers tae a competitor – ye couldna' expect that."

Candles tried a shot in the dark. He sipped his free drink and tried to sound nonchalant.

"I ken, I ken – there's no need tae tell me. They fell off the back of a lorry. That's it, isn't it?"

Traction found this amusing and it was some time before his spluttering would allow him to reply.

"Naw, naw, I can assure you, they didna' fall off a lorry – no, definitely, not off a lorry!"

He continued to laugh; Candles continued to search for the reason for his amusement.

Charles, thinking everyone was friends, returned to his obsession. He moved closer to Traction.

"It's a wonderful thing that treatment," he said pleasantly.

"Treatment," asked Traction, "whit treatment?"

"The trees! That stuff ye dipped them in to keep the needles on the branches and off the carpets."

Traction's amusement increased.

"Oh, aye – that treatment. Oh aye, it's guid, very effective – very simple an' a' – it's jist salt water – that's a' - salt water!"

The truth exploded in Candles mind.

He stood up and glowered at Traction.

"Ye blaggard, ye blaggard, ye unspeakable blaggard. I ken

where ye got thae trees – ye picked them up off the rocks. Admit it! That's where ye got them!

Traction's smile gave way to an expression of holy innocence.

"I canna' deny it," he said, "that's where I got them – and there was an abundant supply. I understand they were washed off a Norwegian freighter bound for the Tyne."

"Ye unprincipled robber," screamed Candles. "They were my trees – lost off the Cornucopia last Saturday – and fine ye ken it. Ye owe me for thae trees. They belong tae me!"

Traction put down his drink and gave the impression that he was considering what Candles had to say. He studied Candles for a while. Candles looked back hopefully.

'Your trees, you say,' said Johnny at length. 'Now remind me what you said the minister says, 'Trees belong to no man. We may plant them, but God giveth the increase'. I think I've got that right, have I no', Candles?'

He then pulled on his cap, wished the barman goodnight and paced his way slowly to the door. When he reached it he turned round to face the three men. Candles waited expectantly - a change of heart, perhaps?

"And peace on earth good will to all men," beamed Traction and went out chuckling to himself.

Original. 1978-9
Revised March 2022.

DECEMBER 24TH 1695

George Home of Kimmerghame kept a diary at the end of the 17th century. Here are three of his entries for 1695:

Tuesday 21st May 1695:

Mar: Turner came and told me her marriage was bloun up at this time and that she would be content to stay that she met with Kath Neilsone who was to come here in her place and she said that Lady Blackadder would be content to take her. Wednesday 22nd May 1695

Kath: Neilsone came hither from Thos Roucheads in place of Ma. Turner who is going away but her marriage is bloun up and she would willingly have staid but Kat: being entered home I could not send her away again so I called for Da: Robinsone who took up a list of the furniture and delivered it to Kath. I find the linen all gone.

Friday 15th November 1695

I cleared with Kath: Neilsone her fea £8; her shoes £1 8s formerly payd. I gave her £7 16s 8d and retained 9sh 4d as her pole (tax).

The story starts here

December 24^{th,} but not Christmas Eve, for had not the Rev Mr Guthrie, minister at Edrom, warned the congregation of God's people only last Sunday not to countenance old popish customs

'Christmas', he had thundered. 'The mass of Christ! We need no mass, no priest, no intercessor! We have access direct to the throne of Grace! We have no need of mass – of Christ Mass; no need of times and seasons for the Lord is with us, always, even unto the end of the age.'

Margaret Turner, housekeeper at Kimmerghame, accepted what her minister preached, embraced the Reformed Faith, had been tested on it at last communion, tested and passed and received the token that gave her entrance to the Lord's Table. Of course she believed it; nevertheless she had had some difficulty with her morning prayers on the bright and cold morning of December 24th. Because of the date the old words of her mother kept intruding; those old words, those old exquisite words, words that garrisoned the heart against the Devil who prowls around seeking whom he might devour. But words not to be used, for this day and the day after were days like any other days, the minister said.

Her master, George Home, is not at home; he is Edinburgh. He will spend the evening of the 24th with his namesake, George Home of Whytefield, seeking redress from the Earl of Home, and to-morrow he will rise from his bed late in the house of Mrs Hepburn in a close off the High Street. There he will share a simple breakfast with Alexander Home and George Kirton, discussing his health with Mr Kirton who is a surgeon, and his wealth (or lack of it) with Al. Home, Writer to the Signet.

Once they have left him he will dress and visit his close relative and near Berwickshire neighbour, Lord Polwarth and his lady, at their lodging and will discover that the lady has rhumatick pains. He will write letters, pick up news in a coffee house about what is happening at Westminster and will send a copy of the proceedings of the General Assembly to his friend, Dr Abernethy of Kelso. But, as a stalwart of the Reformed Kirk, he will not acknowledge the day, nor be pestered by the old words that afflict his housekeeper.

In Berwickshire, at Kimmerghame, the night of the 23rd/24th had been cold, so cold that John Murdo slept with the horses and brought the smell of them into the house when he carried in the water and coal just as the cold dawn was breaking.

It was cold even in the house that morning, very cold. Euphan Johnstone, the bairn's nurse, complained about it when Margaret entered the kitchen. She had kept the fire in the grate all night but still it was cold, lying where she had lain on the floor wrapped in her plaid, and in a blanket too.

"You'd have been colder in the cott," replied Margaret,

reminding Euphan of her privileges. For had she not been plucked from the fermtoun by good fortune and the wiles of her sister, who had persuaded Mr Home to take on Euphan in her place when she left to get married.

Euphan took no notice of the housekeeper and continued her complaint. It was not only the cold, she said; her charge, the master's two-year old son, Roby, had spent a restless night in the box bed. He was suffering from colic, she said, and they should send to Duns for Auckinleck the apothecary.

It was then that John Murdo brought in the coal, water and the smells of the stable. He made up the fire, then the three servants sat down to their porridge, oatmeal scones and weak ale - just as they did on any other morning.

After breakfast, Margaret despatched John to Duns to fetch the apothecary. The unrelenting frost of the last few days had cemented the boggy paths into solid pavements. John would not need the pony; he could walk. It was barely three miles. If he kept clear of the alehouse he could well be back at Kimmerghame by noon.

Margaret had already decided on a journey of her own: she would visit her parents and take them a little something from the laird's larder. But now she would have to delay her excursion until the apothecary had been.

He took his time. A loud man, proud of his profession and scant ability, and, knowing George Home was not at home, he did not hurry. It was well past noon before he arrived. He interrogated Euphan on the bairn's symptoms, prodded Roby until he cried, then prescribed a purge of syrup of pale roses, a syrup he happened to have with him and was prepared to put on the master's bill. He then invited himself to stay for the meal Margaret was preparing, and over his barley brose scunnered the two women with details of the diseases he had encountered and cured.

Thus, the sun was low in the southwest by the time Margaret set out to visit her parents at Betshile. A natural desire, you would think, to visit your parents at this season, but even this instinctive act of devotion would have to be covered in a cloak of mundane duty; she would call at the mill for a furlet of meal and then, why not, seeing she was out, should she not call into Betshile.

They needed the meal, for once again, as last year, the meagre ration left by her master had run out before the year ended. Because of the cold she put on her quilted petticoats and shoes and wrapped herself in her thickest plaid.

As she approached the mill, she heard angry voices. As she entered, William Waddell stormed out of the door and almost bowled her over.

"Tell the master," he spat out at her, "that James Forsyth is a rogue. We have little enough this harvest, and late, without him cheating us, raking off what little surplus we might have had and sticking it in his own pocket."

The miller was not at all concerned by this threat; he greeted Margaret with affected good humour.

"A gripe," he said smugly, "neglects his land, brings me skinflint corn and expects me to multiply it. And should I report him for the guld mixed with his oats? No, I will not do that, even though he abuses me." Then he added,

"And what can I do for you, Mistress Turner?"

His familiarity grated on Margaret. She did not like the man; he was, as William had said, a rogue, a rogue with a greasy face and a greasy manner. She ordered the meal. She would take a pint now; John Murdo would bring the packhorse to collect the rest. It was to be put down to the account of Mr Home in spite of the miller's complaint that he would be laying out the money until the master returned.

It had been a hard year: wet, windy and cold, with the crop rotting in the ground; little of it too, and late, not just for William Waddell but for everyone. It would be a severe winter; hard already; the year not out yet with the harsh months of January and February yet to come. It would be a bleak winter in Betshile, bleaker there than anywhere, a winter of want and hunger. But on this day, although not a special day, George Turner and his wife would eat well. Their daughter would see to that.

The track from Kimmerghame to the fermtoun at Betshile led across open moor, up the hill and down the other side; a mile, no more. Margaret settled into her walk and found it less arduous that she had anticipated. It was cold but clear and the dying rays of the sun wrapped her in a little warmth and gave a little cheer. The pock-marked path felt rock solid underfoot and the frost had conjured the grasses at her feet into a glistening carpet, now mellowing into a quiet gold in the setting sun. As she walked Margaret reflected on the year that had passed.

It had been a testing year, a troubled year, the year she had lost her job and lost her lover. David Jaffrey! The name stung. She tried not to recall his visits to Kimmerghame, bringing the ale he had brewed. She pushed away the memory of her own flirtations and the clandestine meals they had shared away from the knowledge of her master. She recoiled against the feelings that even now welled up inside her, feelings at once tender and painful. And another: of anger, frustration and humiliation - and a face: that of old Thomas Rutherford, the tittle-tattle teller of tales, telling her of Nelly Brack, the hussy at Polwarth. Yet at least he let it out. Margaret Johnstone had known, so had her sister Euphan and both had crowed when Margaret had left to marry her little Duns tailor; even James Forsythe and David Robinsone had had wind of it, but no-one breathed a word – except Thomas, and only after she had made a fool of herself by announcing her marriage!

And after she had recruited Katherine Neilsone to replace her at Kimmerghame! Then for six long months she had found herself skivvying at Blackadder House and sleeping on the floor with the other servants. At the kirk too, stuck on a bench at the back instead of with the master in the Kimmerghame pew. And the smirking and the whispers. And what about David Robinsone's insinuations about the linen? Was not much of it worn and given away out of charity? Did I take it? What about the man who reported it – the factor himself? David Robinsone will be discovered yet. The master has his eye on him. For did not Thomas Rutherford tell me – as he told the master – that David Robinsone is richer than he ought to be!

She breasted the slope and glimpsed cold Cheviot, dark purple against the glowing evening sky. The sight lifted her spirits. The wheel had turned. She had been restored to her old position. Katherine had gone, her six months served. Promoted to Crossrig, if it is promotion! But credit where it is due, she kept the house well – and the linen! God preserve her - and her new shoes!

Margaret made her way through the broom and gorse over the head dyke of Betshile through the rigs, passing the cottars' huts to reach, at length, the small stone cottage of her parents squatting low in its own neat kailyard.

The house felt cold. Beyond the partition steam rose in a cold cloud from the sleeping ox; a broom fire blazed in the centre of the room and sent a lazy plume of smoke wandering up through the crude roof beams towards the vent in the roof.

As Margaret entered, her mother turned from the fire to greet her. The women embraced. Then, from the folds of her plaid, Margaret produced the packet of meal, and added to it a plump young pigeon from the Kimmerghame doocot. Her mother wept as she received the gifts, wept with relief, wept for joy, wept for the day and the daughter that had brought such blessings.

"Our meal will not last," she said. "We had to sell the calf for lack of feed. The harvest was no harvest at all with the rain and the cold. And what little meal we get back from James Forsythe will not store; it is likely to rot. It will not compute; a third for the laird, a third for sowing, a third to eat; but wherewith the tenth for the Lord? It will come from our table and we are like to starve – but for you, my love."

As they spoke, George, Margaret's father entered; with him, Margaret's brother, William. The men greeted Margaret, and Margaret produced for her brother a small, worn, fine linen handkerchief. He received it as if it were a silken shirt. Her father bridled; her mother gasped. She should not do this; these are the master's things, the master on whose goodwill and mercy they utterly depended. If he knew....

"You must only use it in the house," Margaret instructed William. "The master has no use of it," she added to placate her father and mother.

"We will set the light, Mr Turner, now that our daughter has come."

Margaret wanted to object. What would the minister say if he knew? Did he not warn us against superstitions? Especially those of times and seasons. But when she looked into the old work-worn face of her mother and saw in it the determination that had carried her and her family through many a hard winter, when she thought of what lay ahead in the coming weeks: of darkness, of cold, of hard gnawing hunger, of hanging on for dear life, she kept silent and allowed her father to proceed.

The precious coals had already been laid in the fire against the ceremony and were now glowing red. Her father drew them out with a cleft stick and plunged them into a wooden bucket filled with water. The coals hissed and spat as they gave up their heat to the water. Then each of the family: father, son, mother, daughter, sank their hands into the bucket and washed their faces in the fire-kissed water. Then her father picked up the bucket and carried it to the ox to drink. The animals too, must share in the blessing.

When he returned from the stable Margaret's father brought with him the skull of ox, bleached white with age. He then placed a candle inside the eye socket and lit it with a straw from the fire. He then drew back the sackcloth that covered the paneless window and with his family watching he placed the ox skull in the space beyond. There it would give its light to the dark world outside. As her husband set down the skull Margaret's mother intoned the old explanation:

'It maybe that Our Lady Mary and St. Joseph with their yet unborn treasure may come in the night, seeking shelter.'

On her way back to Kimmerghame through the gathering darkness, Margaret imagined still the thunder of Mr Guthrie's denunciation of such superstition, but now it lay silenced by a clear small voice, speaking in her own heart.

'Is it so bad to make strangers welcome? Was not our dear Lord born in a stable? In a fermtoun, maybe, like Betshile?'

When she rose the following morning, in her prayers she

did not hesitate to use the old words: *Christus Natus Est*. Into our cold, dark world, Christ is Born.

December 2013

WILLIAM BRYDEN, MONK

In 'Coldingham Parish and Priory', a book by A. Thomson, I came across an entry from the 1440's that intrigued me. It concerned two 'repentant' monks who had been sent to Coldingham from the mother house at Durham. One of the monks had the name of William Bryden. (The other, John Dorward, was, at the time of my writing, a well-loved doctor in Eyemouth. I balked at using his name!)

*N*ote: *While researching the history of Coldingham Priory I came across a text in the library of Durham Cathedral that may be of interest. It is written faintly on the reverse of a treatise on the Rule of St Benedict, which may account for its being overlooked in past studies. It is written in a curious mixture of vernacular English and Latin and signed with a scrawl that is indecipherable. I have taken the liberty of translating the document into a text more readily understandable to modern readers.*

William Bryden, by the Grace of God a brother of the Mother Church of Durham, for his sins writes this on the Third Day after Christmas in the year of our Lord 1442 at the House of our Order at Coldingham.

Until recently, I had not, I confess, liked my calling. I do not like it now, but I have changed my view of it and find it might be useful, if not enjoyable. I acknowledge that I have no vocation for the contemplative life. I am in it by an accident of birth, being the third son of Robert, of Middleham in Yorkshire - his third son and a great disappointment to him. My brother, Stephen, the first born, inherited the estate. My second brother, Ranulf, found a commission with King Henry the Sixth, whom God preserve; a commission, a diplomatic commission with no other employment than to visit foreign courts and there to cavort with as many ladies as he can, and to attend the army when there are spoils to be had, but not when there is danger; a commission that cost my father a small fortune in bribes; money wasted on that wastrel brother of mine. Holy Mother of God, forgive me for the bitterness I feel towards him. But is not such bitterness justified when the bread is taken out of my mouth to pay for his excesses, leaving me with nothing but a humdrum life of bare cells, scratchy cloth and grey cold mornings, bought by my father with a pittance of an indulgence in the Priory at Durham?

I had, I have, no appetite for monkish work. I do not like prayer; I despise the liturgy; I cannot sing or chant in tune and have no mind to try. I abhor study, do not care for books, cannot draw, carve or sculpt, or execute fine letters in books of vellum. (I write this confession only through the office of Brother Wilfrid, scribe at Coldingham, who is all that a monk should be and all that I am not)[1]. I cannot cook and refuse to clean out latrines, so they put me in the garden and the field. I hate it. I hate the cold soil, the reluctant earth, the sodden fields, the rotting vegetables. Leave it to the weeds as God intended; feed on herbs, wild berries and nuts; kill a boar to eat, or catch a fish; or let some peasant that likes it till the ground; there is more to life than hoeing and holiness. I am not alone that thinks it. Most of the brothers think the same, but only the courageous say it. John Dorward says it, and Robert Knoute, and both suffer for it from Sir Thomas the Prior, hypocrite that he is. He does no work, says no office and is seen only at the Priory when there is someone to impress. He shows no restraint with board or bottle and none in the bed. Go to his hunting lodge at Houndwood if you would hear the truth about Sir Thomas Nesbyt; ask the Forester there what the Prior of our House gets up to in the woods, or the Housekeeper what kind of house he keeps.

I should not be ranting thus, and Brother Wilfrid refuses to write more in the same vein. I have been given the opportunity to mend my ways as if a light has lit up a dark house, or the weather has broken fine after a month of storms, or a fever has been stilled [2]. I must take it if I can, or the few years left to me will be no better than the thirty and three that I have wasted to date and for which I must surely answer before God to my everlasting perdition.

I arrived at Coldingham nine months ago, arriving on the Day of St. Benedict, our Founder, having been sent from the Mother House of Durham for repentance and rectification. Not all the sins laid against me I admit, but I confess now that there were enough of them to merit my banishment to this bleak and inhospitable place. Nor did my banishment much improve me, for I discovered company here amongst the brothers as bad as that which I had left behind. And when we had run through the alehouses of Coldingham we discovered that we were made equally welcome in those of Hiemuthe, a port a little south along the coast. The black robes did not offend them once they knew there were coins in them, and there were women enough who did not balk at the company of a well-furnished monk. Here we used to ....[3]

But all that came to a stop when we were reported to the Superior at Durham (by whom, I would dearly like to know!). Sir Thomas then received a letter putting a sharp end to our enjoyment. Here is it verbatim [4]: *"From credible reports we learn that our brethren, John Dorward, Robert Knoute and William Bryden residing with you wear the garb of religion, but do not lead a regular life of decency of morals, but rather impugn by their acts, the honour of religion. For they, as it is said insolently wander through the towns and villages of the district, and in suspected places, most inconvenient to our order, and conduct themselves frequently before seculars with reproachful words, to the injury of religion, and the scandal of individuals. Wherefore we instruct you immediately to warn the said brethren called before you, that they neither eat nor drink in Coldingham except in your presence; nor go beyond the bounds of our monastery without your special license, the cause of the journey, the place visited, and the hour of return, being truly ascertained and recorded."*

This was a severe penalty and quite unnecessary. We sought only a little relaxation from our prayers and labours. But it was insisted on and for three miserable months I toed the line, or rather, kept my sins close; of which I am not prepared to say more having now repented of them. But come the Eve of the Feast of Christmas, the season of joy, the season when all heaven and earth rejoices, was it not reasonable to seek some enjoyment? The Prior, having taken himself off to court for the winter, so I could not ask him for a licence, and the Sacristan, a dull, formal man would not, I know, have been disposed to grant one, so I decided to license myself a trip to Hiemuthe to the sign of the Swan.

So authorised, I slipped out of the monastery when the holy brothers were at Vespers and took the Law Road. The day was gloomy and the weather bleak; a snell wind blew in from the sea under a sky overcast and threatening snow. Recent frost had broken the ground then yielded. Hurrying feet, trampling hooves and rumbling wheels had kneaded the track into a squelching, slippery quag. But though my feet slithered, my limbs shivered and my eternal soul balked, my mind, intoxicated at the prospect before roistered lustily with anticipation.

Thus, tossed in a crosscurrent of emotions, I made my way slowly along the road. Picking my way through the Paddock Mire the track opened up to Coldingham Bay and I felt in the cutting wind the icy rebuke of conscience. At Fleurs the first flakes fell - from heaven as if it were trying to cover my trespass. On the slope to the Killieknowe, the snow fell so persistently and so whipped into my face, that I could not see the track and several times stumbled from the path: such a parable; such a warning![5] Still I went forward in the dark; afraid to progress, yet howled on by the cry of my intentions. The elements smothered my senses. I could neither see nor hear, the wind buffeted me, the cold robbed me of my breath. When I reached the fermtoun, to recover my wind, I sought shelter in the lee of a crude bothy, a pile of stones and turves with a rough thatch of heather, no more. When my breath returned I thought me that there would be a fire where I could warm myself and, perhaps, a drink that I could force from the peasant. (These country folk are no match for a man of the cloth when it comes to the distribution of God's beneficence! They are easily persuaded that we hold their eternal salvation in our hands. Besides, they are tenants of our House and I have found that if religion does not make them pliable, economics will).

I banged on the door and entered without waiting, ducking low into the low light of the interior. I knew what to expect: an earth floor, half strewn with reeds, crude rafters, bare walls, a shelf or two, scattered pots and pans, a wattle partition separating the complaining cattle from the humans; all lit by a meagre fire and guttering lamps. All this I expected and all this met my gaze. But something more, something entirely unexpected: a Nativity. There beside the fire lay Mary - a poor country woman, half propped up on a low crude straw bed dressed in rough clothes; there Joseph, a labourer, red-haired and hairy-shirted, half risen and turned towards me and there the Baby wrapped in swaddling rags lying at his mother's breast; still, too still.

"God bless you, father; you have come." said the man. "There is no breath in our little boy. We have prayed."

With that he took the child from his wife and thrust him into my arms. I froze. Two faces looked into mine, pleading with me. Something was expected, some words. I tried to recall the prayer for the mortally sick, or that for the infant dead, but could remember neither. I gabbled what came into my mind: "Venite, Exultemus Domino" then rattled through the "Litany", which I have often parroted but little to my benefit, the meanwhile rocking the baby in my arms. Then, a miracle! How else can I describe it? The bairn let out a loud sigh, followed by a sob; it wriggled in my arms as if reaching for life. I muttered, "Jubilate Deo", and handed the child back to the mother who put him to her breast. As he started to suck, she bent her head and kissed him. Her husband stirred the fire then knelt beside her. The fire flared; the oil lamps sputtered, the beasts in the byre lowed and moaned.

When the storm lifted I did not go on to Hiemuthe and the Swan, but turned back to Coldingham, puzzled but strangely elated. As I came over the Law the clouds lifted, the moon came out and the Church bell pealed in the birth of Christmas Day. With me I had a shank of ham, a thank offering.

At the Priory I am popular: with the holy monks because of the miracle; with the roistering brethren because of the ham. But I care not for adulation. I am a changed man, and see plain my calling: it is to the poor; I will no longer prey on them; I will be their shepherd[7]. Christus Natus Est.

1. I suspect these words, whilst written by Brother Wilfrid, were not dictated by Brother William. This is one of a few passages where Brother Wilfrid probably wrote what he thought rather than what Brother William said.

2. Surely "as if" ......to......."stilled" is another of Wilfrid's flights of creativity. We know from a poll roll of monks in 1445 that Wilfrid regarded himself as a poet.

3. Here the text descends into garbled dog Latin of which I can make no sense. We must assume that here Brother Wilfrid, offended by the words dictated to him yet fearing the wrath of Brother William if he refused to write, scribbled anything that came into his head.

4. Would William want his rebuke publicised in this way? I think I detect Brother Wilfrid's voice again and it is a smug voice; we can almost hear the holy joy. Was Wilfrid the scribe who penned the Letter of Reproof, or even the perpetrator of the original complaint?

5. Killieknowe is now better known as Hallydown from Helig (Holy). Is it fanciful to speculate that Brother's William's "Miracle" is the root of the name?

6. Surely Brother Wilfrid again.

7. It may be of interest that, in my research of the Coldingham Chronicles I came upon an entry for 1446, recording a plague that swept through the villages of Coldinghamshire. Three monks from the Priory are reckoned among the dead having caught the plague from "going amongst the people during their affliction". One is a Brother William.

Christmas 2007

CHRISTMAS COUNCIL

Coming out of the Maltings Theatre in Berwick the eye is assaulted by a bulky coffin-shaped building blocking the view to the town's elegant Town Hall.

There was no need for the Gainslaw Borough Council to meet in the week before Christmas. They had no business to transact and no decisions to be made. But how else could they justify the Gala Christmas Dinner if they did not have a meeting immediately before it? The meeting resembled no other in the year. For one thing, councillors looked forward to it.

Of course, there were some who looked forward to all of the meetings - the talkative ones, those who liked to hold the floor and demonstrate their dramatic abilities, councillors like Jack Robson. But Jack Robson would not be at this year's December meeting, due to the fact that he had died in October.

As we shall learn, that event spoiled this year's Christmas meeting, and the Grand Dinner left a sour taste in the mouth. Not that the borough's representatives regretted the absence of Councillor Robson; the vast majority were relieved he would not be there; he had the irritating habit of asking awkward questions.

Normally, the Christmas dinner conditioned the meeting before it, warming everyone into the best of humours. Executive and opposition contrived civility if not harmony, the agenda was short, and business kept to those items the councillors might know something about. The dinner itself would be a sumptuous affair set in the gracious old Guildhall graced with chandeliers, gleaming cutlery and waitresses in black frocks and white aprons.

This year, however, the Christmas meeting got off to a bad start:

'Item 1. Minutes of the last meeting: all agreed they are correct record.'

No, not all.

"Item 13, Mr Mayor, Redevelopment of the Blackett's building".

"Your concern, Councillor Collingwood?"

"The minutes state that the council expressed the view that the site should be developed in keeping with its proximity to the Guildhall."

"Yes,"

"Does that statement not suggest that the Blackett's building was not in keeping, and that the council may have been complicit in its destruction?"

"In what way?"

"It is well known that the Civic Society have long disliked the Blackett's building and are now relieved that it has gone. If we insist that the new building is different from the old building does that not mean that we are tacitly agreeing to its eradication? May that not place the council in an invidious legal position, particularly in light of the circumstances of the building's demolition? In short, Blackett's might sue us."

"Come now, Mr Collingwood, surely not. What is the alternative?"

"That the building be replaced in its original form."

"But it was hideous!"

"Nevertheless, better that than being accused of orchestrating its replacement."

"Point of order, Mr Mayor,"

"Yes, Councillor Jackson,"

"We are supposed to be agreeing the minutes, not discussing the substantive issue."

"Of course, apologies. The minutes, are they a correct record of what was determined at the last meeting?"

The Mayor surveys the nods and shrugs of the assembly.

"There seems broad agreement that the minutes reflect accurately what was said at the meeting. Agreed."

"Councillor Collingwood has a point. We must not give any appearance that we condone what happened." Councillor

Chalmers.

"That doesn't follow." Councillor Jackson again.

"But that's the way it looks. I certainly don't want anyone to think that I had anything to do with it."

"Order, order! The minutes! Are they a correct record?"

"Permission to raise the issue under any other business?"

"Do we have to?"

"We'll be here all day at this rate."

"Councillor Collingwood, would you oblige us by raising this at next month's meeting?"

"Yes....."

"Good."

"...provided the minutes of the current meeting record my reservations about the minutes of the last meeting. I don't want....."

"Yes, we know...."

"I believe there are others who wish to be dissociated from any appearance of condoning what happened to the Blackett's. We could find ourselves....."

"Councillor Jackson, did you say something."

"I was just thinking aloud. There are some of us who wonder how the building got the go-ahead in the first place..."

"I hope you are not implying that there was something unconstitutional anent planning consent. I was new to the council myself at the time but can recall nothing that ....."

"Mr Mayor, we are not discussing the Blackett's building – just the minutes....."

"Of course. Alright, alright. Is there anyone else who wishes to be associated with the motion?"

"What motion?"

The Mayor consults with Ms Chief Clerk.

"The motion that expresses reservations about the minutes of the last meeting. Item 13: re-development of the Blackett's Store Building. Are you in favour?"

Nods.

"Show of hands. Ms Clerk, record the names of those

voting."

A hand goes up, then another. Then those not voting look round; they see hands raised; the tide is running against them, more hands, then more, until all hands are raised.

"Agreed that the minutes of this meeting show that the minutes of the last meeting do not reflect the wish of the council to be disassociated with the demolition of the Blackett's building?"

"Agreed. Next business".

Items 2 to 8 passed on the nod. Only one item to go, then home to prepare for the Gala Dinner.

Item 9: Appointment of this year's Citizen of the Year.

"You have had the list of nominees and a short resume' Could we have a nomination please? Councillor Jackson?"

"I believe, Mr Mayor, that it is customary to award the accolade to any councillor who has died in harness during the year, but I see that our late colleague, Councillor Robson, is not on the list of nominees."

'I would have thought that was obvious,' snapped Councillor Collingwood. 'In the circumstances, we could hardly make Councillor Robson Citizen of the Year. That would really put the cat among the pigeons."

'Not obvious at all,' answered Councillor Jackson smoothly. 'We know there were accusations, but nothing has been proved.'

This statement brought sighs and groans from most of the councillors.

'Come on, Bruce,' exclaimed Councillor Collingwood, 'we all know what happened.'

'Forgive me, Raymond', purred Councillor Jackson, 'but I, for one, do not think we should blacken a man's reputation until it is proven beyond all doubt.'

'Giving the man the benefit of the doubt is one thing,' put in Councillor Chalmers, 'but honouring is quite another. I think we would do the man more favour if we just drew a veil over it.'

This brought murmurs of impatient agreement all round.

"Nevertheless,' began Councillor Jackson, 'if we don't

nominate Adam. . ..

The Mayor banged down his gavel and, showing every sign of satisfaction, shouted 'Order! Name!'

''Apologies,' murmured Councillor Jackson, 'Councillor Robson, this year, we will not have the opportunity next year.'

Then he added,

'Point of Order, Mr Mayor, seeing that Councillor Robson is no longer with us, is it correct that the name rule applies to him. After all, when we all come to appear before the great tribunal in the sky, will we not be addressed by our 'Christian' name? Isn't that what it's for? Besides, when Councillor Collingwood addressed me by my Christian name, or, should we say, forename, you did not rebuke him.'

The Mayor glanced towards Councillor Collingwood, lifted his gavel, flinched, then put it down again.

Councillor Collingwood stood up and bellowed at the Mayor.

'Mr Mayor, how long are you going to allow this charade to go on? He's up to his old tricks.'

The Mayor stared at Councillor Jackson and opened his mouth. Before he found any words to utter, Councillor Jackson jumped in.

'May I suggest away forward, Mr Mayor? Could I suggest that you allow me to bring forward a nomination for Councillor Robson to the next meeting. We can then discuss it without the threat of the Christmas Dinner hanging over us?'

The Mayor stared at him for a few seconds, then glanced at Councillor Collingwood, and the other impatient faces in front of him. Seeing only signs of weary acceptance, he banged down his gavel and pronounced,

'Agreed. Meeting closed.'

I am sure you will want to know what Councillor Jackson submitted to the January Meeting. Here it is.

I wish to nominate Councillor Adam Robson as 'Citizen of the Year'.

Adam E Robson served as a conscientious and hard-working

member of this council for thirty-two years until his much-lamented death earlier in September past. In his time, he has chaired many of the committees of the council, including finance, transport, and social services.

But it is as an outstanding convener of the Building and Planning Committee that he is best remembered. The town is indebted to him for fine examples of tasteful renovation of our historic buildings. A quarryman by trade, he supplied, free of charge, many of the Whinstone blocks, used in the restoration of our town hall, a beautiful building of national, if not international, interest.

In making this nomination, I feel that, because of rumours circulating in the town, I must address the issue of the destruction of Blackett's store. Certainly, we know that Councillor Robson hated it, and declared that its erection, thirty years ago, had formed one of his reasons for joining the council. But then many townsfolk disliked the building, and cannot understand how such a building received planning permission. It constituted a blot on the townscape. When viewed from the south and west at any distance, near or far, its brutal bulk blocked the view of our elegant Georgian town hall.

Such was his dislike of the Blackett's Building, and, having failed by any legal means of replacing it, I do not doubt that Councillor Robson may have occasionally, in jest, threatened, to bring a little something from the quarry to blow it up. Indeed, I have it on good authority that he had been heard to promise that he would do just that, were he to be told that he only had days to live.

That he received such a verdict on his health in August is no proof that he was responsible for the explosion that wrecked the building in September.

I therefore ask the Council to disregard these suspicions and award Councillor Robson the accolade he so richly deserves.

The Council, unsure of its legal indemnity, and afraid of offending the business interest, turned down the nomination. However, if you visit the Town Hall in Gainslaw you will see an elegant raised bed, full of flowers. It is made of Whinstone and carries this inscription:

'*From the townsfolk of Gainslaw, to Councillor Adam Robson, in gratitude for his courageous and dynamatic contribution to the integrity of our town.*'

And you may think that the signwriter has slipped up with his spelling.

Or, perhaps, not.

Christmas 2022

COAL, CHRISTMAS AND A
SKIPPING ROPE FOR SALLY

In her eighties, my mother agreed to record memories of her childhood. Born in 1899, She lived with her family at Hebburn Colliery, where her father worked. This story is based on what she told me, though not necessarily at Christmas. I have used the real names of her family.

"Coal, we will have plenty of coal, now that father is at work again. We will have warm fires this Christmas, if nothing else."

These were Sarah Jane's thoughts as she built up the fire for the bairns coming home from school on that bleak December day in nineteen hundred and six.

She would have plenty of coal, for the Wallsend and Hebburn Coal Company would provide it free. Not out of charity; it was part of the deal that kept her husband tied to Hebburn Colliery whose gigantic winding wheel loomed over the house. The house, too, belonged to the colliery.

It was not much of a house: two rooms and a pantry downstairs, two rooms upstairs. No running water; no power either, except that provided by the fire - and the oil lamp she now lit and set on the scrubbed wooden table in the centre of the room.

But Sarah Jane was happy with 3 School Buildings, happier than she had been a bare month ago. Then she had faced Christmas as a dependant of her sister Elsie in her cramped terrace house a mile away in James Street, hard by Palmers' Jarrow Shipyard. Trying her best, Elsie would do her duty by her sister out of love, but finding you need more than love when you have three adults and seven bairns sharing a two-bedroom upstairs flat.

Sarah Jane had had her four daughters with her but not her husband, Tom. Not that he had not been invited to James Street, but there was scarcely room for him and he was not prepared to shove in with relatives. His independence lay close to the heart of him. It had carried him into the pit from school, had raised him there from boy's work, putting and driving, to man's work, driving the seam and clearing out the stone, to the very pinnacle of the profession – numbered and honoured among the hewers; the men who cut the coal and made the money for the rest. Such a man, you will understand, would not easily accept another man's accommodation.

He also suspected that Elsie and her husband James blamed him for the distress of his family. Of course, they did not accuse him to his face, but they were sure in their own minds and conversations where the blame lay.

Not with Waltham, the Colliery Manager, they thought. He was just doing his job as he saw fit. Tom had a way of rubbing up the bosses, and it had cost him his hewer's job when the downturn came. He had showed some sense when he took on the stoneman's job when things picked up but had not shown much gratitude. When there was a fall of stone that Sunday and Tom didn't show up, you could understand why Waltham had thought that he was back playing games with him, that Tom still resented not being offered his old job back. You could understand, then, why he sacked him.

Even then, we think that Tom could have sorted it out; could have gone to Waltham and explained that he had been away to his uncle at Kibblesworth to borrow money to tide them over, now that the dole had stopped and that he would get no pay for a fortnight. We're sure if he had gone to Waltham and explained it, had eaten humble pie, and pleaded for his job, he would have been taken on again.

We're sure that would have happened. But no! What did he say to Sarah Jane? 'If he wants me, he comes looking, I don't go cap in hand to any man.'

What Sarah Jane thought about her husband's intransigence, Elsie never discovered, nor will we, for Sarah Jane uttered not one word of reproach. Do not call her subservient. She was never that, but she understood what Elsie and James did not: that Tom, for all his determined self-belief, needed someone at his back - and had she not promised she would do that for better or worse back there in the little Methodist chapel at Hetton.

Now the 'worse' was over and they were restored to their own house. The manager had come looking for Tom; not Waltham, but the new man needing good hewers, men who knew what they were doing, men who could kirv and nick, who could hew and fill and do it efficiently; men like Thomas Thompson, he was told.

Now Sarah Jane faced Christmas, on Wednesday, with a light purse. Her Tom, out of either thoughtlessness or recklessness, had spent most of his last wage buying a silk scarf for her and a chain for his father's watch. A celebration, he had told her, of better times.

'And what about the bairns,' she had replied, 'what are we to give them?'

'They'll have their time,' he had said, then added, 'you'll manage; you always do.'

So, on the Saturday evening before Christmas, the whole family, father, mother, and the four girls, set off for Ormonde Street in Jarrow a half a mile away, dressed in the best they could manage. Best of them all walked father in his suit with waistcoat, watch and chain, and a brushed bowler on his head.

Before you rush to rebuke this cocky man for his swank, consider this: he hazards his life every day; a thousand feet below ground in one of the most dangerous pits in the country; in a darkness you cannot imagine, pitching his skill and intuition against the looming threat of explosion, stone fall and crushing, with only a pick in his hand and a lamp at his side. In the ten years he has been at Hebburn Colliery eighteen men have died down the mine. In truth he owes his restored prosperity only to the death of too many hewers in the past two years; good men, men like Peter Bradley, and big Bob Chalmers; men he knew. And Jacky Bramwell last week, killed at the face by a fall of coal on the shift after him. You would not deny him a watch chain and a bowler hat to wear to the shops on a Saturday evening, would you? Sarah Jane, in spite of her protests and empty purse, cannot bring herself to resent it and is wearing her new silk scarf when she sets out for the shops

Ormonde Street, on a Saturday evening, is greedy with shops eager to relieve the bustling throng of men, women and children of their hard-earned wages. Tom strides off to stand with other bowler-hatted and suited workmen in the street, with miners, shipyard workers, labourers and others, to swap stories and opinions and weigh up, either openly or secretly, their comparative prosperity.

Sarah sends the girls window-shopping. She must make this Christmas, as she has made the past twelve Christmases, a wonder for her family, this time with scarcely any money. She will therefore set out to scrape together something to add to their stockings on Christmas morning. (She has already knitted gloves and scarves and has scrimped a silver threepenny bit for each of them to find with delight in the toe).

She trawls through the shops, setting aside her poverty, determined to make her scanty provision run as far as it can. She buys tangerines, apples, a bag of nuts, a candy stick for each of them, crayons and a cheap colouring book they can all share. She adds something special for each of them: a jigsaw for Ethel, a hairbrush for Mary, her oldest now ten, a set of little wooden animals for her youngest, Edith. But what to buy for Sally? What would Sally like? What can she afford? A doll? No. A tinplate toy mouse? No. A bright book of nursery rhymes. No, all too dear! A ball? Yes, a ball, a bright red ball.

The following day, Sunday, the whole family walks along to the end of the row to the Primitive Methodist Chapel. The mother and father will sing and give thanks that they have reached another Christmas without disaster or disease. They know that there are those there that have not been so fortunate, such as Michael Holmes, Deputy Overman, from Quality Row and his wife, who a few short weeks ago nursed their little son and lost him to scarlet fever. Fearing infection of grief if not of affliction, some in the congregation are wary of them, but Sarah ushers her girls into the pew beside the Holmes's and Sally finds to her satisfaction that she is sitting beside Polly, their daughter, a girl of her own age who has brought along a new bible with pictures in it.

In the service, Sarah, hoping God is listening, prays for the safety of the unborn child she is carrying. And God willing, could it be a boy, not only for her husband's sake, but also to provide for them when Tom can no longer do so? Or is that selfish?

When Tom, black from the back-shift, came home on Christmas Eve he found a blazing fire and his home decked out for Christmas. It is the work of his wife and children. The bright chains hanging from the ceiling were made by the girls, and they have gathered ground ivy from the staithes by the river to put behind the pictures - of Mother and Son, the horses on the moor; of the Clipper Thermopylae; and of their mother's favourite, a silvered rendition of Gainsborough's Blue Boy. Paper lanterns, made by the girls, festoon the brass rail on the mantelshelf, and the chenille cloth that covers the mangle has been covered with stars made from silver paper. In the centre of the white scrubbed table, underneath the glowing oil lamp, lies an exquisite cloth bright with embroidered red and gold flowers, a gift to Sarah Jane from the lady and gentleman of Hetton Hall when she left their service to marry Tom.

But even such a rarity could not outshine the 'mistletoe' hanging in the window recess. Sarah Jane has made it from the hoops of an apple barrel, two hoops intersecting each other at right angles to create a hollow sphere, then covered with tissue paper, hung with streamers, and now bearing little chocolate coins covered with gold paper.

His walk from the pithead through the bleak pit yard may have been cold and dark, but when Tom took the door of his home, its brightness burst on him in a wave of light and warmth – admiration too for his wife, and yes, (though he would never admit it in Ormonde Street on a Saturday night), of love, love for Sarah Jane and his daughters.

How could Mary and Ethel, Sally and Edith be expected to sleep with such excitement in the house and empty stockings hanging on the bedpost? They snuggled in from the cold and chattered until their tongues ached; they watched and waited until their eyes drooped, then listened in the darkness until sleep overtook them.

Sleep came, too, to all of School Buildings, to Quality Row, to Oak Street, Elm Street and Ash Street and to all the other houses and terraces clustered round the great hulk of the colliery. The great winding wheel also slept that night, for no men would be roused from their beds by the knocker-up in the small hours of the morning. And children restless in their beds would not mistake their calls for that other visitor they longed to hear.

'Has he been?' the voice of Edith, calling in the dark morning to her sisters. A scurry out of the clothes to the foot of the bed, to the stockings hanging there. Their expectant hands reach, grasp and are filled.

'Yes! Yes! He's been! He's been!'

Molly lights the candle. The house bursts into life as the girls explode into their mother and father's room, clutching their stockings and presents. Edie has already started on her candy stick.

'He's been! I've got a jigsaw, look, mam, a jigsaw!'

'I've got a hairbrush!'

'A zoo, a zoo!'

'What has he left for you, Sally?' asks her mother.

'I have a ball,' says Sally holding it out for her mother to see. But the hand that held it trembled – with disappointment, Sarah Jane suspected. There was something else Sally had wanted. What was it?

But no questions now! It is a time a rejoicing.

'Back to bed,' orders their father. 'You'll catch your death of cold, it is too early. Go back to bed.'

Back to bed! Attempted, but impossible. After half-an-hour, Sarah Jane rises, descends and lights the lamp and the fire. The girls throw on their clothes and tumble down the stairs in her wake. Tom comes last and sniffs a cold morning as he replenishes the coal bucket.

Ethel settles to her jigsaw, Edie sets out her animals on the floor, and Molly having brushed her hair takes Sally onto the staircase to play with her ball. She sends Sally to the top of the flight to let go the ball as she attempts to catch it at the bottom, as it leaps and bounces towards her. Then Molly at the top and Sally down below.

But Sally's heart is not in the game and the staircase is cold and dark. Soon they are back in the kitchen with porridge on the table.

Then a squabble and Sally the cause of it. Ethel has commandeered the colouring book and is attempting to colour in one of the pictures. Sally wants it, and shouts that it is her turn. Then grabs it; Ethel retaliates. The book is on the floor; Sally on her knees is leaning on it with all her weight. Ethel is trying to push her off. She nips Sally. Sally hollers. Mother descends and takes the book from both of them.

'What's the matter with you?' she demands.

'She doesn't want her ball,' explains Molly. Sarah Jane looks at Sally.

'Do you not like your ball?'

'Yes,' replies Sally, 'but......'. She bursts into tears.

'She wanted a skipping rope,' says Molly.

'I asked him for a skipping rope,' Sally sobbed, looking doubtfully at her mother.

Sarah Jane put her arm round her daughter and whispered,

'Run across to Mrs Holmes to see if she has one'.

Sally did not need a second invitation. She dried her tears, scuttled out the door, across the yard, into the street and down to Quality Row. She knocked at Mrs Holmes' door; Polly opened it and let her in.

'Mrs Holmes,' said Sally, half in hope, half in fear, 'mam said to ask you for a skipping rope.'

Mrs Holmes looked at the little girl and smiled.

'Polly,' she commanded, 'fetch the clothes line!'

Polly brought the clothes line.

'Stand up straight,' Mrs Holmes ordered Sally. Sally obeyed. Then Mrs Holmes pulling out the rope measured Sally from head to foot, then drew out the same length again. Then she cut the rope, tied a knot in each end of the cut length, and gave it to Sally.

'There you are,' she said.

Sally took the rope from her and skipped her way back home to her mother and sisters.

That was how Sally got her first skipping rope. At least, that is what she told me eighty years later.

And learnt, into the bargain, that there is more to Christmas than Santa Claus.

Sarah Jane did give birth to a son, Bob. My mother remembered the doctor coming on a bike to deliver him.

December 2014

ALBERT, MADONNA AND
THE BIG BASS DRUM

This story hails from my Singer days, when I regularly drove through Drumchapel. This sprawling estate had been built after the war to house people being cleared out of the old tenements closer to the centre of Glasgow. Some parts of Drumchapel were pleasant; others not so. And that included the largely neglected shopping precinct. But where there's a need there's the Salvation Army.

The child stood close to Albert in the Concourse most of the afternoon. The Concourse! The bleak centre of a bleak housing scheme: some bright councillor's bright idea now faded and decayed.

Some attempt has been made to lighten it for Christmas. Those shops not yet boarded and blind have decorated windows. Frenetic lighted bulbs chase round and round the square balanced on rickety poles; a scrawny Christmas tree sprouts from a hole in the cracked pavement, flapping its meagre branches in the thin wind.

Then, as always on the afternoon of Christmas Eve, the Salvation Army Band has played carols for a couple of hours. Band! Four songsters in bonnets, a small huddle of brass in navy raincoats - plus Albert on the big bass drum. Such a small band needed no big drum, but Albert has played the drum since he joined the Army forty years ago, ever since he was plucked from a life of sin by the Grace of God and the perseverance of the songster who became his wife. Now, with the band diminished and his wife gone to glory, the brass allow him to thump along – but quietly, with restraint, and not at all in the gentler carols. But, on this afternoon, whether he thumped or kept silent, the child stood by him in the chill wind.

Albert recognised the little girl from her eyes, black almost, peering out of a pale face. He had seen her go past his gate to school, and had spoken to her when she leaned over the gate to watch him tend the rough grass and scrub privet that counted as his front garden. But he did not know her name or where she lived.

She was, he thought, about seven years old. He had smiled at her now and then that cold afternoon, and did not think she could be warm enough in her faded pink anorak, brown tights and mealy-pink woolly hat. In one of her mealy-pink gloved hands, she held on to a plastic bag from ASDA.

Then, finally, *"We wish you a Merry Christmas,"* a rallentando of brass, a roll on the drum, and the performance concluded. A few hearers, pausing momentarily between shops, clapped their gloved hands momentarily – and silently.

The tubas, euphoniums, cornets and songsters left the Concourse, climbed into their cars, and went off to enjoy the Festival in merrier parts of the city. But this was where Albert lived - a few hundred yards away, along Councillor McClutchey Walkway, among the stark towers and terraces of Drumry Ridge. The child stood by him, had patiently observed the break-up of the band, standing there in the square as if she belonged to Albert.

"Time to go home," said Albert, looking at the child. "Is your mammy in the shops?"

"No, she's at home."

"You are here all on your own?"

"I'm with you," she said.

'That cannot be', thought Albert immediately.

"But you need to go home now."

"What time is it?" asked the child anxiously.

Albert looked at his watch.

"It is just after four o'clock."

"I can't go home yet," said the child. "Me mother said six o'clock."

Me mother! Not 'me mammy'! Not Glasgow, not Scots –

English, broken English, foreign? East European?

"Six o'clock," repeated Albert to give him time to think, "Do you have somewhere to go until then?"

"We are strangers," she said, fixing her eyes on Albert.

'Strangers! No! I cannot accept that. There must be someone!'

"What about your father?"

"I have no father."

"What is your name?"

"Madonna."

"Well, Madonna, where will you go now?"

The child shrugged her shoulders.

"Could you not go to a neighbour? Or a school friend?"

"Me mother said wait here. She is coming for me at six o'clock. But I'm cold and it is dark. Can I not come with you?"

'Can I not come with you? Do not ask me! Please do not ask me that!'

"I can carry the drum."

Albert laughed to cover his confusion. She would carry the drum! It was all she could offer! He put his arm round the child's shoulder and pulled her to him. A shock ran through him. Was it the glance of the woman who was passing? Did she not pause for a moment to inspect him? Yes - and more than that, much more than that - forty-two years of it - in the old life. He separated himself from the child. He could do no more for this child. He must leave her in the Concourse.

He took her to the door of ASDA and told her to wait, told her that her mother would come for her - and told himself that she would be safe there, in the doorway; plenty of light, plenty of people, beyond danger. After all that is what her mother had arranged; she had not arranged for her child to attach herself to the big-bass-drum player of the Salvation Army band; she was no worse off than her mother had intended.

He said goodbye as cheerfully as he could manage, but the child did not reciprocate. She gazed at Albert, her eyes expressionless, her lips pursed, her quiet face upturned towards him.

He must go. He picked up the drum, turned and walked away from her. When he reached the gap in the shops that opened onto the Walkway, he turned. Instinctively. He did not think it advisable to turn, knew he would be sickened by what he would see - the little girl standing in the doorway, in her thin anorak, brown tights and mealy hat, clutching her ASDA bag as if it were her failing courage. Looking at him! Betrayal!

But when he turned he saw immediately that she was no longer alone. Three lads had surrounded her, two of them hooded. One of them had grabbed her ASDA bag and was tugging at it; the others were hustling her into a corner, screening her from any passer-by until the bag could be ripped from her. Albert did not hesitate; he put down the drum, shouted and ran back to her. The louts fled. He grabbed Madonna's hand.

"Come with me," he said, angry at the bullies, angry at her mother, angry with himself.

He led her out of the square into the gloomy Walkway and along the littered path through scrubby shrubs and stunted trees towards Drumry Ridge, that part of the sprawling estate that housed both the girl and himself.

He would take the girl to her home - to the address she gave him, to 2/8 Lomond Court, 2 being the block, and 8 the top floor back, up the common stair. The drum made the climb clumsy and Madonna's help proved not all that helpful.

He put down the drum, rang the bell, and withdrew his hand from Madonna's grasp. She let go reluctantly then tucked herself between the drum and Albert and waited for the door to open. No-one came. Albert rang again. After a few moments and another ring, the door opened a fraction and the face of a young woman, a young, pale, heavy-eyed woman, peered out of the narrow gap. When she saw the uniform and the child she re-closed the door, removed the security chain and opened the door wide. She was dressed in a loose shift, floral, creased. Albert immediately suspected that the dress alone covered her nakedness, and instantly knew why Madonna had been sent to the Concourse.

"Madonna," she said, then spoke to the child in a language Albert did not understand. But he understood what she said next, for it was meant for him: *'Why did you run off? I have been worried about you.'* Albert sensed that this mother had done this previously, before other symbols of authority. Madonna made no move to enter the house, but stood clutching her bag, half-hiding behind the drum.

Then a voice from inside the room: male, Scottish, coarse.

"Tell him to fuck off," it shouted.

"Poliza!" hissed Madonna's mother.

After a short delay, a hard-faced, half-shaven, flabby-bellied man, dressed only in a pair of trousers, appeared behind the woman.

"Naw," he exclaimed, "that isn't the police; he's the Sally Ann and, Christ, he's brought his big drum." He guffawed, then continued.

"The wean'll be alright with him. Get rid of him. Here, give him a quid!" He thrust a pound coin into the woman's hand. She passed it out to Albert. Albert refused it.

"Your child....," began Albert

"Fuck off!" shouted the man, "and take the wean. This is no place for her. Bring her back the morn. But leave the drum at home - we can do it without music!"

He guffawed again. Albert studied Madonna's mother's face and read a tumult of emotions: fear, mother-love, self-loathing, despair. She gabbled something to the bairn and shut the door.

Albert made to ring again then stopped. The brute is right; it is no place for a child; he could not leave her here. He picked up the drum, took the child's hand and turned away. Then the door re-opened and Madonna's mother thrust a plastic bag into her child's hand, glanced at Albert, muttered "Please!" and shut the door.

'*Would she have done it,*' Albert thought, '*had I not been in uniform?*' The uniform, his witness to the world that he was Christ's true soldier, had deceived a mother and made a hypocrite of him.

'*What can I do now? When I reach home I will contact Social Services and tell them about the child. That is what I must do! I will ring as soon as I get home home; before she takes her coat off! There will be an emergency number, surely. But is that wise? What will they think of the mother? Of the child?*'

'*Of me? I have been with the child alone now for over half-an-hour. Plenty of time to.........*'

'*It was impossible! No, not the Social Workers! I must take the child to my home, keep her there for the night and return her to her mother in the morning – and tell the mother what I think of her, and that she should get help. I could put her in touch with someone in the Army; they would help her to sort her life out. No! I cannot do that; I cannot keep the child alone in my house. No!*'

He would take her to Mrs Harrison, a few doors away, a good Baptist, well-respected. She would take the child. Madonna would be all right with her.

On the way to Albert's house, they carried the drum between them, Albert bearing the weight, Madonna holding on. They walked through the gloomy streets, under teetering tower blocks, past garages hideous with graffiti, between gaunt houses. But Madonna saw only lighted trees in windows, dangling Santas climbing walls, and spectacular displays of reindeer, shooting stars and hanging balloons. Every now and again when her courage rose sufficiently she gave the drum a sharp tap, then looked at Albert, half-guilty, half-afraid, brave. She was, Albert thought, quite happy, expectant; against all the odds, trusting in Christmas. But he would have to let her down; she had not yet reached the stability she longed for. He could not give her a lodging; she must go to Mrs Harrison.

To Albert's house: 15 Mentieth Avenue; not an avenue at all: a unit-built, pebble-dashed tired terrace on a narrow street once lined with trees, but now only with cars whose wheels had reduced the grass verges to rutted mud. Albert opened his front door but did not allow Madonna to enter. He lugged his drum into the small entry and left it there, then re-locked the door and, taking the child by the hand, walked her two doors up to number 19, to Mrs Harrison.

He rang the bell. No answer. He rang again. No reply. He went to the window and peered in. The room lay in darkness. He came back to the door and knocked on it. A door opened. But not Mrs Harrison's - the adjacent door: no. 21, Mrs Sutcliffe, English, nosy, gossipy.

"She's away for Christmas to her son in Castlemilk."

She glanced from Albert to Madonna.

"And who is this then?"

Albert hesitated only a moment.

"My niece's little girl. They are here for Christmas."

A lie, a blatant lie, in the uniform of the Lord, a lie.

"Happy Christmas, Albert"

"Happy Christmas, Mrs Sutcliffe."

'Why did I lie? What else can I do?'

"Come along, Madonna, you will spend Christmas with me."

It horrified the child that Albert had so few decorations, and, after a tea of fried pizza, spent the evening putting up streamers, tree, baubles and balloons that Albert fetched from the loft. So doing, Madonna raised the house to a brightness Albert had never known, for no child, not their own or any other, had lived there, even for a night. It had always been avoided.

Meanwhile Albert prepared the back room for her, made up

the bed and put a hot water bottle in it.

Then they sat down together to supper, during which Madonna told him about her school and her classmates, but not about her home. Then the child went to the bathroom and on to her room taking with her two plastic bags, the one her mother had given her containing her nightie and toothbrush, the other the ASDA bag she had held onto all day.

After she had gone Albert filled one of his socks with any bits and pieces he thought might please the bairn: a few sweets, a chocolate biscuit or two, a satsuma, an apple, one or two coins, a model car he found in a drawer, a pen and a pencil, and a Christmas Card, on which he was about to write his name when he changed his mind and signed it from Santa Claus. He taped the sock to the mantelshelf in the living room then sat for a while by his electric fireside and contemplated his foolishness.

For foolishness it was. How often in his testimony at the Citadel had he talked of the old life: of drunkenness, of waywardness, of petty theft and casual sex. The mention of casual sex had shocked some members of the Corps, but not his wife who knew and understood that he was a changed man.

She knew, too, about his conviction, though no one else at the Corps knew for he had never admitted it, not in all the testimonies to the saving love of Jesus, not in all the years, his conviction for molesting a child, a young girl. That is all – molesting; not rape, not underage sex, not violence of any kind; just drunken excess, vaguely remembered – even then: pulling the frightened child to him for a kiss; admitted at the time; unimaginable now; regretted every day for forty-two years.

But a conviction, nevertheless, long time-lapsed and struck off by Limitation, yet brooding behind the door of the old life – until now. And these days, he knew, the law did not forget such offences. There is no escape in the past, no old life and new life, no act of Redeeming Grace for such a person. (Even in his thinking, the common label frightened him, and he could not use it; a label now attached to him until his dying day).

'*Would Madonna's mother, feckless as she is, or even the brute, have allowed me to take the bairn had they known what I am?*'

How foolish to bring the child home and keep her for the night. It is not true that he could do nothing but give the child a bed in his house. He could have contacted Social Services – in spite of the consequences for mother and bairn. For him it would have been safer. He could have contacted the Army; they would have collected the child and given her a home for the night in one of the hostels or refuges. He could have contacted the police, or one of the songsters.

But he had not - and he knew why.

'*Because I want to keep the bairn for Christmas. Because, in spite of the threat and horror of discovery, in spite of the disgrace if I should be caught with a small girl in the house, I want her in my home at Christmas. It is time to face it. It is proper, it is right, it is loving, it is Christian. It is simple enough: like Mary two thousand years ago, Madonna needs a bed for the night, and I have one.*'

Thus comforted, Albert went to bed and was soon asleep.

He awoke to a thumping in his head. He looked at the clock: ten past six. The thumping materialised into the beat of his own drum. He put on his dressing gown, hurried downstairs and found Madonna banging on the covered drum with her hand.

"Happy Christmas, granddad!" shouted Madonna, when she saw him.

"Happy Christmas, Madonna," said Albert, "but shush now. You will wake the neighbours."

"Happy Christmas," repeated Madonna and handed him the ASDA bag she had hung onto all yesterday.

Albert hesitated. Surely she had bought whatever was in the bag for her mother. Now she was offering it to him. Should he accept it?

He took the bag from her. Watched closely by the little girl, he lifted out its contents: a bar of Dove soap and a bag of Liquorice

Allsorts.

"Thank you, m'dear," he said, "thank you. But I think we should give the soap to your mother, d'ye not think?"

Madonna shrugged her shoulders, her face expressionless.

"And," he added, "somewhere I have holly paper; you can wrap it up, if you want."

Madonna nodded her head and smiled.

"But I have nothing to give you," smiled Albert.

"You could let me bang the drum," said the child.

"I could indeed," replied Albert.

He took the cover off the drum and handed her a drumstick.

"Gently now," he said. "It doesn't have to be loud."

Madonna took the stick and with obvious delight banged the drum. Then she turned to Albert.

"You must sing," she said.

And Albert sang:

Hark the herald angels sing
Glory to the new born King
Peace on earth and mercy mild
God and sinner reconciled.

Christmas 2010